The True History of Dragons and Wizards

James Pesavento

Books by James Pesavento

Book two in this series
The History of Dragons and Wizards:
The Spawn of the Hellkite

The True History of Dragons and Wizards

THE LORD OF THE FORMS

Pesavento Publishing

Published by James Pesavento
Cover Design by Marcia Diamond
ISBN: 978-1-7377799-0-2

Table of Contents

Prologue . . . . . Page 1

Chapter 1 . . . . Page 2

Chapter 2 . . . . . Page 20

Chapter 3 . . . . . Page 31

Chapter 4 . . . . . Page 39

Chapter 5 . . . . . Page 44

Chapter 6 . . . . . Page 46

Chapter 7 . . . . . Page 49

Chapter 8 . . . . . Page 52

Chapter 9 . . . . . Page 55

Chapter 10 . . . . Page 57

Chapter 11 . . . . Page 63

Chapter 12 . . . . Page 66

Chapter 13 . . . . Page 76

Chapter 14 . . . . Page 81

Chapter 15 . . . . Page 83

Chapter 16 . . . . Page 85

Chapter 17 . . . . Page 90

Chapter 18 . . . . Page 95

Chapter 19 . . . . Page 102

Chapter 20 . . . Page 107

Chapter 21 . . . . Page 114

Chapter 22 . . . . Page 118

Chapter 23 . . . . Page 124

Chapter 24 . . . . Page 128

Chapter 25 . . . . Page 131

Chapter 26 . . . . Page 136

Chapter 27 . . . . Page 142

Chapter 28 . . . . Page 148

Chapter 29 . . . . Page 154

Chapter 30 . . . . Page 156

Chapter 31 . . . . Page 162

Chapter 32 . . . . Page 166

Dedication

To Muktananda, my teacher.
He allowed me to experience the world's true magic

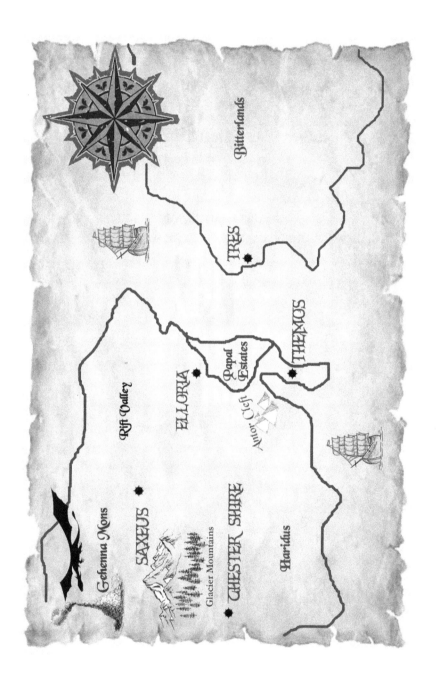

Prologue

History is a story twisted by the victor. They whittle the truth to carve images of heroes and villains. Characters are recast. Motivations are reforged. Plots are rewritten. The ignoble are made noble and the defeated are defiled.

A hundred years from now there will be no eye witnesses. People forget. Memory is fickle. Stories àre embellished. The generations that follow will only have the songs and legends to relate this history. If left to time, what remains will be a false narrative, a distorted chronicle. This account is as true a narrative as I am capable. It has been transcribed so that an eon from now people will remember.

Chapter One

The fleshy walls were touching every side of me. My mind was gripped with claustrophobia. I was trapped within a cocoon, a watery prison. I heard a steady beat. There were muffled, indecipherable sounds from far away. Month after month, locked in my confinement, a form grew around me. It was relentless. Day in and day out it grew and wrapped itself over me. I witnessed my metamorphosis. I could only observe as I became something alien.

Panic overcame me. I could no longer relent to this powerlessness. Within that limited space, I flailed and kicked. My leg broke through the fleshy wall and the lake around me drained. I thought I would flow with it but I remained trapped. The pressure was crushing my foreign body. It felt like a dream, a nightmare. One foot started to make its way out and then the other. I could feel the cool air. Suddenly my legs were grasped and I was dragged through the tunnel. The glare blinded me. My body was bruised and bleeding, but I was free. I could breathe.

I was swaddled in rags and taken away. I never saw my mother. Her experience was beyond what her small body could bear. I do not even know where she was buried. It was December 1349, the year the black pestis had killed more than ninety percent of the people in the surrounding villages. Bodies were no longer individually buried.

I was born, my mother died and my life unfolded in my aunt's house. She named me Simon. I was now her son. My cousin Thomas became my brother. We were better off than most. I was greatly loved by my new mother and brother. I remained undamaged and was spared the pangs of hunger. I would always be an orphan. I was not destined to become an urchin or a waif.

In my second week I was baptized, now bound to things eternal, to the one truth, the one Power. I would belong. I would be accepted. I would be deemed worthy. Most importantly, I would be saved. It was granting salvation that assured the church would endure and hold sway. Church power was engrained in all aspects of our life.

The one room that was our home was crafted from an ancient bluestone, quarried hundreds of years ago. The rock held inclusions that sparkled and splashed flecks of light against the walls whenever the sun came through our window. I marveled at the beautiful light that dappled the room with glittering diamonds. We had our own fireplace. We could cook our food inside and stay warm.

My brother Thomas was strong, muscular and big boned. He was two years older than me. He looked like a man. His teeth were straight and white; an exception. His hair was thick and black. Thomas loved to eat and his favorite pastimes were mischief and sleeping. As he was approaching his eighteenth birthday it was considered unusual that he had not yet married, but then Thomas was never in a hurry to do anything. His preference was to be with his mates rather than experience the uncomfortable awkwardness of being pursued by a flirty girl. Thomas was loquacious and lived engaged with people. He could meet someone new and within five minutes they were his friend. He was the provoker, the instigator.

I, on the other hand, lived on the outskirts of life. I did not enjoy engaging with people and preferred to be by myself. I was thin, tall and fair. People described me as lanky and withdrawn. I was either working or thinking, but never resting. I was perpetually curious and wanted nothing more than to explore by myself. I lived in my imagination. Sleeping, conversing and trouble-making were not my ideas of fun.

Thomas was always happy to be the rascal, the champion, the protagonist. I always looked upon him as my protector. He gladly accepted that role and for that I was grateful. He preferred to assist our mother in the baking and they carried on long conversations. I preferred to chop the wood, outside, in silence. My loneliness was persistent. My island felt safe and required fewer defenses. Loneliness is never simple. It becomes your creator or your destroyer.

My aunt never spoke of my father. One day I asked her directly, "Mother, would you tell me the story of my father?" She answered, "The peace of this land and our very existence is because of the courage of your father." She would say no more. I assumed he had died and it was too painful to recount. Maybe he was a war hero. Left to my imagination, that story felt better than abandonment.

She loved us above all else. My aunt was named Claire Baker. The current Lord of Chester Shire had requested she become the head baker for his estate but, being fiercely independent, aunt Claire politely refused. Her masterful baking skill allowed our family great stability and we never lacked for food, love or necessities.

We lived in the heart of Chester Shire. It was a grand farm, encompassing an entire valley, owned by one family. The current owner was Lord Loefwin, the great grandson of Lord Chester. Most men worked for his family. Throughout planting and harvesting seasons we too worked for his Lordship. Thomas enjoyed the hard, physical work. I always found my mind wandering off, seldom fully engaged with the labor. I spent many hours daydreaming as I worked in the warm sun.

There are many stories of land owners abusing the serfs under their control. The gentry were frightening figures that treated their helots like animals using them to till their soil, build their homes and chop their wood. Lord Leofwin was the exception. He was kind.

Chester Shire had been protected. The black pestis had ravaged the four villages east of Chester Shire but our land was spared. Tales of death, disease and famine in the four villages circulated throughout our shire and fear of the pestis turned everyone into pariahs. People wouldn't travel to other villages, fearing exposure. Strangers were shunned. The inhabitants of Chester Shire were now leading isolated lives.

Villagers believed our shire had been unharmed by the ravages of the pestis because of the wizard, Ailwin the blue. He was of legend and no one from our village had actually encountered him. My aunt taught me the songs of his deeds, as do all mothers. The songs recount how Ailwin had rescued the king of Elloria from the Huntsmen who lived in the Bitterlands of the Far East.

The songs say that Ailwin wore a vest of dragon leather and was considered a seer. The legend said that Ailwin had retired to the Glacier Mountains north of Chester Shire.

The foothills of the Glacier Mountains are covered in rolling fields and forests of great red oaks. In the spring wild honeysuckle blooms, wafting over the hillsides, filling the air with its sweetness. Their flowers are considered a delicacy but the berries are poisonous. The red oak trees are majestic and several have girths as wide as a house. They produce a profusion of acorns which are slightly bitter. When boiled and roasted they are an important source of sustenance. My mother said that in ancient times there were silver oaks with leaves that sparkled like precious metal when the sun shone upon them. They held great medicinal properties. The silver oaks have long disappeared but there still exist cherished pieces of furniture made from their perfect wood. They are considered masterworks and greatly treasured.

My mother also related stories about the great forests of the Glacier Mountains that made Thomas and me shiver with fear. In the most northern reaches of the Glacier Mountains lies Gehenna Mons, a towering volcano that to this day throws fire into the sky. Tradition says that so much fire and brimstone fill the netherworld that the earth cannot hold it all and occasionally the earth is required to make room for more devils by tossing the molten earth into the air. The legends say devils and dragons live trapped within the confines of the Sheol underworld where the dead go to practice the necro-arts. Somewhere near the base of the mountain is the entrance to the netherworld inhabited by demons.

I always believed these stories were fabrications narrated to prevent children from going there and getting lost in the dark woodland. I thought the stories were manipulative fiction. Some parents would scare little children into being good by threatening to send them to the Sheol and never return for them.

When you remember everything, you are very different. I realized my experience was unique. This added to my sense of detachment. I would speak to Thomas of things that happened when I was one or two years old. Thomas, even though he was two years older, remembered few of those events. I considered Thomas quite clever. He could whittle tools, find cagy ways to get us out of trouble and was resourceful whenever we were in scrapes, but I held the memories. I witnessed everything. I felt removed, marooned. I was a watcher.

It was a week before my 16th birthday. As winter approached the work in the fields had wound down and there was free time. There were barely any leaves left on the trees and a chill inhabited the air. This was a prelude for the impending grip of winter's gelidity. Far in the distance the Glacier Mountain tops were showing the first tinge of white.

I found our town's isolation confining and longed for adventure. I was yearning for exploration and, if in the course of my adventure I could discover if the fearful songs and legends were true, all the better.

I addressed Thomas, "Brother, tomorrow I will set out for the Glacier Mountains and discover if the lore is true. Our whole lives we have lived confined to this valley. The outside world has remained a mystery. It is time to reveal this enigma."

Thomas, at first, wanted nothing to do with dark forests. It was in the forests that the devils and the Formorians lived and wielded their chaos. But when he saw that I was going whether he accompanied me or not, he relented and knew he must go.

We packed a two-day supply of cabbage, elderflower and rosewater cheesecake, and spinach pie. We would be at the base of the mountains so we dressed in our winter wear of woven wools and felted hats. We wore our dark brown, high leather boots to keep the mud from soiling our garments and thistles from puncturing our skin. I selected my favorite walking stick; the one Thomas had carved with symbols for my fifteenth birthday.

At our age we were considered men so our mother would no longer question us. With the first light of dawn appearing on the horizon and the sky flushed with pink hues we headed out the door. The chill made our noses run. Because I was thin, the cold easily found its way to my bones. I did not like being cold, but that inconvenience would not stifle my adventure.

In Chester Shire the fields are rich because every spring the river floods and covers them in new soil. New soil is highly prized. It allows the cabbage, spinach and wheat to thrive. Apple, pear and walnut trees flourish. The river is abundant with fish; pike, roach and carp being the most abundant. Rising from the land that surrounds the fields are the rolling hills that are blanketed with grass, emerald green in the spring and golden in the fall. These grasses smell pungent and fresh and every fall we would shave the hills with our scythes and sickles to produce hay for the stock animals to eat in the winter. Here the pigs and chickens are kept and the cattle and sheep graze. The grazing areas hold an earthy smell. On the northern horizon looms the great mountain range. This land was my home. It felt pure.

Lord Leofwin did not allow people to throw waste into the streets, streams or fields. As part of his faith, he believed in being tidy and clean. He loved the earth for he knew it sustained us. It was into this cherished land that we set out. As we began to walk down the muddy road Thomas said, "Simon, do you not fear the Formorians?"

I responded, "They are not real. Those stories were made up to prevent us from exploring the forest and keep us in fear of punishment and damnation."

For a moment Thomas considered that but then retorted, "But the Formorians are always in disguise and appear as the great storms, the winds that blow down the trees and the lightning and thunder. They are great gods."

"Thomas, if they were gods they would have no fear of mortals

7

and would show themselves. I promise, if a great storm begins to brew we will return quickly."

My pace was quicker than was comfortable for Thomas so I purposely slowed to a more appropriate gate. Every hour Thomas would ask if it was time to rest and eat. I was constantly being pushed onward driven by sheer enthusiasm. For me this was a stimulating research expedition. Out here I was free. For Thomas this was performing his duty of protecting his little brother, mixed with a degree of reluctance and trepidation. The topography was always moving higher, the opposite of what Thomas preferred. Soon the trail disappeared and within a few hours we were left blazing our own pathway through the tall brown grasses.

Forests of massive red oaks appeared. Thin wisps of fog wafted through their limbs. The gossamer strands of misty clouds reminded me of watching the men in the shire pub smoking their meerschaum pipes, their rising fumes snaking into the hazy air. Sporadically the mist would brush against our faces and cool our brows. We rested under an impressive bough of a monumental red oak and filled our bellies. After satiating his hunger Thomas laid down and within 30 seconds he was fast asleep. I needed to relieve myself and walked from the forest's edge into its deepening embrace. I was about to return when I noticed a soft blue light in the trees. My heart beat faster and my usual imperturbability left me. I was about to flee when a man appeared between two monolithic trunks.

He was tall and thin with pure white hair. His face held deep lines but he stood tall and upright, with energy, with power. His skin was soft, not weathered by sun or wind or worry. His eyes possessed depth and clarity. They allayed my fear. His white beard portrayed experience and knowledge. He wore deep blue robes edged with gold brocade and a vest embroidered with black dragon leather. He spoke quietly, "You have finally come. Now is the time to begin."

Fear left me. I was wonder-struck, mesmerized by the soft blue light that surrounded him. That light felt warm and peaceful. My mind stood still. My legs did not move. I asked, "How do you know me?

What needs to begin? Who are you?"

"I am Ailwin and there is not much time. Come. I am old and there is much to do."

I protested. "Thomas will awaken soon and if I am gone it will worry him."

Ailwin was impatiently focused on one outcome and, at a near run, he headed toward Thomas. I followed. Thomas heard our footsteps and awoke suddenly, sensing the quickening pace of two people approaching him. Ailwin reached down and stroked his head. In a soft monotone he whispered to Thomas, "It is time for you to return home. A great storm is coming. Simon is staying and I will protect him. He will return in three days. Go now."

I fully expected Thomas to push him aside, grab my arm and make us return home together. But Thomas simply nodded and walked over to me, hugged me and whispered in my ear, "Simon, if you are not back in three days I will come for you." I nodded and Thomas departed. That was so unlike Thomas that it seemed surreal.

Neither Thomas nor I understood what was happening and we did not seem to have any desire or will to resist it. When true power is being wielded, its intention manifests.

I wanted to go with Ailwin. I was drawn by the stillness of his presence and the soft blue light that surrounded him. Maybe it was my insatiable longing to search out the novel, the unique, the interesting. Those facets of life had been kept from me because of my age and circumstance and I yearned for them. Maybe it was the sheer excitement of being young, naive and inquisitive. Whatever it was, I was filled with anticipation and exhilaration. I was on the brink of adventure.

I picked up my walking stick. Without speaking, Ailwin and I walked into the forest. My mind seemed only capable of forming questions. There was no fear, no worry. I simply followed AIlwin, waiting to understand why there was so little time and what was so important to do. He turned his gaze toward me and said, "Quickly now. The darkness is rising."

It felt as though what I had unconsciously known my whole life was about to be revealed. Either that or I was under a spell. Either way I did not care. I should have felt dread but all I experienced was freedom, eagerness and the never-ending questions my mind produced.

After several hours the rolling hills covered with red oaks gave way to spire rocks and pines. We ascended into an area of sharp crags and steeper climbs. The sky was filled with billowing white clouds. The air continued to become brisker. Finally, Ailwin stopped, faced the rock side and spoke one word, "Ipentur."

Neither a door nor an opening appeared. The rock face before us began to glow with sparkling light. He grabbed my arm and we walked through the effervescence. It felt like warm fog on my skin. The space we entered was cavernous, alleviating my fear the cave would be claustrophobic. On both sides of the entry stood massive crystals of light blue, translucent Celestine, rising over twice our height. They terminated in standing points and filled the windowless room with soothing light. On the far left a stream of water issued from the rock and flowed into a small pool which overflowed, disappearing into a sink in the rock floor. To the right the larger portion of the great room was furnished with wooden tables, chairs and two beds made from perfect silver oak. The chairs and headboards were richly upholstered in azure blue cambric. The wooden legs and arms were intricately carved with symbols. I only recognized one symbol. It was one Thomas had carved into my walking stick. It was attributed to the Formorians. With that realization the spell of contentment was broken. I whipsawed from inquisitiveness to panic. Fear gripped me. My body became hot and sweat formed on my upper lip. My heart began pounding.

Ailwin watched as I surveyed the symbols. He said, "We only fear what we do not understand. Sit." He handed me a cup of water and I sat in the chair he motioned toward. I could feel the energy of the place as I sat. It seemed to envelop me in stillness. I continued to feel my throbbing heartbeat. I felt out of time and space, as if I had been transported inside a dream.

I impulsively asked, "Are you a Formorian?"

Ailwin responded, "You are addicted to questions. Formorians are people who remember. They are the wizards who see. You call Formorians gods and you fear them or you deny their existence because you have never seen one. I only reveal myself in the time of trials when discretion and anonymity are no longer possible, when I can no longer remain nameless. When the times requires it, I come forth to restore the Balance."

"What Balance?" I asked.

"You live with the pairs of opposites. You live with good and evil, love and hate, happiness and sadness. Throughout history, humans have demolished civilizations to birth empires of greed. Good crumbles and evil rises. When evil, hate or anger begin to dominate, the Balance must be restored or cataclysms ensue. Left imBalanced, the time of humans could end. Balance is the role of Formorians."

He continued, "You arise from the Formless and when you remember you are the Formless you become a Formorian with all the powers. The Formless is your nature. It is who you essentially are and the Forms are the powers you access when you remember. You always hold that power but you have forgotten and experience separation. Then you have no access. Forgetting is why humans suffer. You are here to remember."

"Remember what?" I asked.

He showed a faint smile and answered, "Remember you are essentially Formless. All people are potentially Formorians but only a few of us can access the Formless. You have the powers within you. You have always had the powers. A Formorian realizes the Essence, accesses the powers and wields the Forms. You are a nue', a novice, but you are one who can remember. That is why you have been chosen. Only a nue' who is capable of remembering can see the blue light. Most humans are incapable of seeing the Light of Essence and only see the outer expression of the Forms, but you see. Enough questions for now. It is time to eat and then you will sleep."

11

Ailwin always ate in silence. In fact, he spent most of his time in silence when he was not training me. That night I slept soundly despite the hundreds of questions spinning around in my head. As I awoke I smelled the sweet aromas of fresh almond fritters and cabbage soup. We ate. Food never went to waste.

Throughout breakfast I fantasized about wielding power. I would command the dragons and be a great wizard. I would have a name that evoked power. I expected Ailwin would start this morning showing me how to do this. Instead, he sent me to my chair and said, "Sit in silence." Two hours later he said, "Come. We will go into the forest."

He brought me to the edge of a high rock cliff that overlooked the Valley of the White Deer. A soft zephyr blew over us as we sat at the cliff's edge. The smell of pine scented the breeze. We sat on the brown grasses in silence.

After several minutes, Ailwin spoke, "A thousand years ago, the Balance reigned. The air felt that harmony. Rains were sufficient. Winds were clement. Men were wise. Life and death played out in equilibrium. For centuries that Balance held sway. Slowly, over time, men began to forget. History was twisted. Chivalry was supplanted by a struggle to rule. The Balance was lost and men sought power. Throughout much of the Earthlands fear has grown wild. Some men now eat this fear and fill themselves with cruelty. A few still struggle to remember.

For the past two hundred years the dragons have multiplied and ravaged their domains. Men fought to keep them at bay. The church put bounties on their heads. New weapons were forged to pierce their scales. Whole armies were created to limit their incursions. And still their shadow grows.

Power is now held through fear. Outcomes are achieved though ruthlessness. In our tenebrous time, the Balance is distorted and thousands die. Still, there are lands where the Balance is held in place by the Forms."

I was hesitant to respond but after a great pause, unable to contain my questions, I asked, "Teach me first to protect my family?"

He let out a laugh that echoed down the valley. He looked at me and said, "Nue', you seek power but can't even sit in silence."

I protested and said, "I didn't say a word for two hours. I did as you asked."

Ailwin didn't appreciate my protest and in a quiet, firm tone said, "Your tongue was mute but your mind raced, never once silent."

I acknowledged, "Yes, but I have no control over my mind. I cannot fix that."

He said, "It is not about fixing yourself. When you know you are the Formless your mind will be silent. Then your mind can wield the Forms."

Within hours he had destroyed my fantasy of being a wizard by the time I returned to see Thomas in two more days. My name was not a name of power, but Nue' which connoted a novice with a lack of knowledge. My beginning was not auspicious. Dejected, I asked Ailwin, "How do I know I am the Formless?"

"So many questions," he said. He rose and stood before me, a looming presence. I could tangibly feel his mien of power as he reached for me. He held my head in his huge hands. They felt warm. His thumbs pressed firmly onto my closed eyelids. In seconds my body, from head to toe, was filled with energy. Currents of power coursed through me. I thought the pressure from his thumbs would crush my eyeballs and I would be blind. Then the thought arose that the immensity of the energy would burn me to ashes. But I felt no real fear. I held no resistance. I surrendered. After one minute he released me. I sat motionless. My mind had stopped. My breath had stopped. The boundaries between what was inside me and outside me disappeared. There was only me everywhere, unrestricted, unfettered, free. The questions ceased. There was complete stillness. I do not know how long I sat in this state before he said, "This is silence. This is remembering the Formless."

We returned to the mountain and I had no desire to do anything except hold that experience. I wanted nothing to disturb the exquisite stillness. In sixteen years, I had never experienced a silent mind. But Ailwin prodded me and made me prepare dinner and clean. As soon as my work was completed he sent me to bed. I went to sleep slightly disgruntled from the interruption.

The following morning Ailwin required me to prepare breakfast. I made mushrooms with leeks and one of my favorite foods, apple fritters. As I cleaned up he petted his cat, Filidae. I still felt unsettled and unworthy. I silently lamented that I was being treated like a slave serving the lord of the manor. After the meal was over I inquired, "Are you going to teach me the Forms?"

He furrowed his brow and said, "You don't get it nue'. You don't learn the Forms. You remember the Formless. You always have the powers within you but right now you remain separate from their Source. When you remember you are the Formless, separation ends and the Forms act as you need or will them. That is what wielding them means. When I touched you yesterday and you felt the descent of power, you experienced separation ending. You were still. When you are in stillness you remember you are the Formless. In those moments of stillness, you had access to all the powers. You were able to see. The Forms stood at your ready. When your dissatisfaction arose afterwards you lost your realization. Come. It is time to go to the Circle of Irminsul."

We walked for two hours through the forest of great red oaks and pines. There were squirrels gathering acorns everywhere making their final preparations for the winter ahead. Our trek took us through a woodland dappled with light and perfumed with the smell of vanilla and moss. Red and yellow leaves blanketed the forest floor. Suddenly the sky opened up and sunlight became abundant. There appeared seven massive silver oaks arranged in a perfect circle. The sun turned every leaf into a glistening jewel. I had never seen a silver oak before and the interplay of the sun and leaves made the entire circle seem magical, alive with life. The place held a power that was palpable. We walked into the center of the tree henge, sat down and waited without speaking. After several minutes Ailwin suddenly rose and turned toward the western side. Silently, a great grey wolf entered the circle and lowered its head as it approached Ailwin. I stood.

Ailwin acknowledged the beast with a nod and the wolf began to shapeshift. Ailwin signaled for me to come. I was hesitant but trusted Ailwin was in charge. The wolf had morphed into a man of 32 years with perfect features outlined by a short black beard. He wore golden robes lined with diamonds. Ailwin addressed the wolf-man, "My friend, this is Simon. Please inform him about what is transpiring in the Earthlands."

Rarely had Ailwin used my name. He had always called me Nue'. In two days, I had gone from the simple life of being a wood cutter, a baker and a child and entered into an unknown land with an unknown menagerie of powerful beings. They were intent upon seeing some grand plan unfold. Somehow I was to have a role in this.

The shapeshifter began, "I am Pargus. It is an honor to meet Ailwin's nue'. Sit beneath the Irminsul trees. The four villages east of Chester Shire were ravaged by the pestis and are gravely suffering now. There were not enough people left alive to even plant the fields this past spring and so, as winter approaches, food is non. More will die. I fear that the pestis was not by chance nor was it a punishment for our sins as the church claims.

The four villages, two mining towns and the port of Themos on the far eastern shore are now patrolled by the Ussyro dragon, Drakantos. She is nesting and in the process of creating hatcheries in the fields surrounding the four villages, filling them with her embryos. She is creating armies of offspring. Ussyro dragons always have masters and Drakantos serves an unknown master. Your village has been protected by the Glacier Mountains and Ailwin's grace but I fear this is not to be for long. Soon all the Earthlands will be affected."

Pargus paused and Ailwin began, staring at me intensely. "The Earthlands are anchored in the east by the port of Themos. Themos has grown powerful as a result of its monopoly of haberden salt cod and pickerel pike. Even when the crops failed the fish were plentiful.

Since the pestis, even as the population declined, the fish business remained lucrative because crops were not sown in the year of the pestis and fish served as the mainstay. Themos has grown wealthy and powerful.

If you approach Themos from the west you must first pass through Antor Cleft, the only practical passageway through the low mountains. Emerging from the eastern side of the Cleft you are greeted by the Myros pyramid. It holds dominance over the countryside and towers over any other structure, even taller than the great church spires of Themos. The Myros pyramid existed long before records began detailing the history of the region. It rises over four hundred feet and its lower three quarters is comprised of over one and a half million blocks of red granite. Its top quarter is composed of blue Celestine which can blind your eyes if stared at in the mid-day sun. For centuries it has served as a beacon for land and sea travelers.

Despite the fact that the pyramid lies close to the entrance of Themos, both the Saxeuns and the Ellorians claim its viziers designed and oversaw the building of the structure. In truth, four thousand years ago the Formorians built it using the power of Forms. The Formorian wizard, Myros, abides in the central chamber to this day. Themos was the first sacred city of the ancient Formorians. It was constructed during the age of Sat when Formorians populated the area in great numbers.

The pyramid remains completely intact with no stones missing. There are historical records that detail how Ellorians replaced blocks that were disturbed centuries ago by grave robbers. One thing is not in doubt. No person who has entered the pyramid has exited it. Ancient spells protect the monument even as each generation tests the sorcery, to their regret. Even the Ussyro dragons will neither perch on its top nor fly directly above it.

Ussyro dragons generally remain in the far northwest, inhabiting the land of Gehenna Mons. The land is warmed year-round, heated by the fumaroles emerging from the massive volcano. Dragons despise cold. They flourish in the sulfuric fumes emitted from the sleeping giant. They perch themselves around the caldera rim to warm themselves with the rising heat emanating from the crater's magma that boils in its lava dome. They scrape their claws on the hard basalt rock, sharpening them into razors. They incubate their embryos in the warm fissures." Ailwin became silent.

The stories about devils, Formorians and dragons that I had repudiated were true.

Pargus said, "Hidden at the base of Gehenna Mons is the opening to the netherworld. Years ago, Ailwin sealed it, its exact location now forgotten except by the dragons and Formorians.

Several small dormant volcanos lie in the shadow of Gehenna Mons. Their ridges have been stripped, denuded by the north winds that blow fiercely in the winter. It was in these ridges where gargoyles and vultures interbred generations ago becoming the vulgoyles that now comb the skies hunting for carrion. Much of the forest has been desecrated by the dragons as they relentlessly pursue their prey, breaking trees and leaving trails of destruction behind. It is a land that has been defiled and sullied, left for the vulgoyles to pick at its bones. The only beauty surrounding Gehenna Mons is the large shallow lake that fills with mating flamingos who eat the red algae and turn a beautiful pink. As the flamingos push their beaks through the water foraging for algae they send countless ripples across the surface causing the lake to sparkle pink in the sun.

Ussyro are the only dragon species in that area now. They have stout, three-horned necks and a mouth filled with serrated teeth that come to needle points. They are generally less belligerent than other species. Their cousins, the Xyro, were sealed within the underworld years ago. Xyro are fearsome. They have two long, thin necks emerging from their torso. Both of their heads are dominated by teeth that are razor-like and extremely long. The scales that cover their bodies are tipped with small blades that curve outward ready to cut the flesh of anything that dares touch them.

The Ussyro that now perch themselves on the caldera's rim are waiting for the netherworld to open and for their Xyro cousins to return. Ussyro dragons make low hissing sounds, mimicking the sound of the sulfuric steam rising through the volcano's vents. It is said they are calling for their cousins to return. It is a land that gnomes and humans avoid. The noxious fumes, the dragons and the knowledge that the devils from the underworld are close by keep humans and gnomes at bay."

Pargus turned toward Ailwin and the two walked to the edge of the circle and spoke quietly. Pargus shifted back into wolf form and walked toward me, bowed and walked out of the circle into the forest of red oaks. Ailwin and I returned to his home in silence. I feared for Thomas and Aunt Claire. I was glad that the volcano remained far to the north. My mind felt overwhelmed, filled with revelations.

On day three I awoke to the same routine. I made a breakfast of salmon pastries and honey crisps and then Ailwin asked me to sit in silence. I said, "The world is being destroyed and my family is in peril and you want me to sit in silence? We need to do something."

Ailwin very softly said, "Unless you learn to be the Formless you will have no ability to wield the Forms and you will be destroyed by Drakantos. The dragon has roamed unopposed through four villages, two mining towns and the great port of Themos, and a baker will represent little opposition. 'Doing' is not what will empower you. Being the Formless will."

And so, I sat. Ailwin sat. Sitting with Ailwin made my mind stop. In the stillness, what was inside and what was outside became one. We sat for the entire morning.

After a small lunch he took me to a clearing near the river and told me to collect wood. I made a small fire. He said I should sit and warm myself. He instructed me to close my eyes and be silent. He said, "Become the Formless". Then he said, "You wield the Forms through your intention. Intend the wind Form to blow."

In the stillness I intended the wind Form to blow. In one second a powerful wind arose and blew the sparks, ashes and embers from the fire onto me and then in another second the wind was gone. I was left running around brushing coals and live flames off of me. I was covered in ash. A few small holes had been burned into my woolen shirt. Ailwin laughed hardily and I realized I was a running around brushing coals and live flames off of me. I was covered in ash. A few small holes had been burned into my woolen shirt. Ailwin laughed hardily and I realized I was a nue'.

Ailwin handed me his kerchief to wipe my face and then we both laughed. He began, "Now you are beginning to understand. We will go back to the mountain and in the morning you will go to Chester Shire and practice being the Formless. I will call for you when the time comes."

Chapter Two

I returned home to the relief of both Thomas and Aunt Claire. While they wanted a recount of my time away, Ailwin had instructed me to avoid explanations. I went about my life as usual but spent my nights practicing being the Formless. Ailwin had wisely forbidden me from wielding the Forms.

I also repeated my prayers each night before bedtime. The fate of my eternal soul rested upon those prayers. My faith was lacking but I was not yet willing to risk eternal damnation and abandon it. My mind had never resolved how a loving God could throw his creation into the flames of Hades for all time, no matter what sin they committed. I would leave the resolution of that for a later time. There were more pressing matters at hand. Adventure awaited.

Rumors had begun circulating through Chester Shire that the situation in the eastern villages had become untenable. Lord Leofwin had ordered food to be sent. Aunt Claire, Thomas and I baked extra loaves and cheesecakes to be sent. Everyone hesitated going near those villages for fear of the pestis. But they were viewed as familial lands and some overcame their dread to journey there, leaving the foodstuffs at the town's edge.

We celebrated my sixteenth nameday with cheesecake. It was a joyous day with family, food and laughter. In our family, birthdays were especially loved in part because it meant celebrating with cheesecake, Thomas's and my favorite.

The next morning the sun shone brightly and the air was brisk. As was my morning routine, I went to the well for water. Pargus appeared and said it was time to return. He was matter of fact and there was no welcome or joy in the meeting. I brought the water back to the house and told Thomas I was leaving and didn't know when I would return. He wanted to go but I said no even as I silently wished he could accompany me.

Pargus the grey and I returned to Ailwin's home in the mountain and as we approached the rock wall I uttered, "Ipentur". Only the lower right corner of the rock face effervesced. Pargus put his hand on my back. I could feel his presence and power as the entire wall face began to sparkle. We walked through.

Ailwin hugged me with a silent bear embrace and we immediately ate. I was anticipating much news but, of course, no one spoke. As soon as the last morsel was swallowed Ailwin began. "I will train you before you make your journey to Elloria. The excursion requires you to traverse the Glacier Mountains. With winter approaching the passes will be closed. We will remain here preparing until the first sign of spring arrives. Then you will set off."

In my impatience I spoke, "But the dragon will smite my village if we wait."

Pargus chimed in, "Simon, Ussyro dragons move slowly in the cold and they seldom fly in the winter. Their embryos are incapable of hatching in frigid weather. Their progress will be slight over the next several months. Whatever game is afoot is a long one."

Ailwin spoke to me, "You saw how the entrance to the mountain responded to your command? You have much to learn. Your intention must become focused. You must be able to be the Formless and to wield the Forms before you leave."

Day after day, from morning until dark, Ailwin tutored me throughout that winter. He reminded me each day that my attention must not falter. Every day he reminded me of the dominion formula, "Stillness makes us Formless. Intention moves The Formless into Form. Understanding is what manifests."

The first few days were a disaster. I created havoc. It was a repeat of my first day with the wind form. On day one I wielded the fire Form. I achieved but a few sparks. On day two I wielded the air

Form. I commanded the wind for the second time and blew Ailwin to the ground. He did not laugh this time. I had only succeeded in putting a scowl on his face. On day three I wielded lightening. I was remarkably good at wielding lightening. I could wield both the intensity and direction. That was enjoyable and encouraging although I did not like the ensuing thunder that accompanied it. Loud noises always unsettled me. I looked to Ailwin for his approval. He remarked, "We all seem to have our particular affinity with certain Forms."

Soon I relaxed and began to listen closely to what Ailwin taught me. "Nue', you still want to be powerful. You are still attached to the outcome. As long as it is about 'you' your access is impeded. The Forms are intelligent. They know your intention and if your intention is clear and held with focus the Forms will attend to your intention. If your attention wavers the Forms feel your lack of connection and retreat. If your stillness is disturbed then you lose your state of the Formless and you become separated from it."

I asked, "Are the Forms limited to the elements like wind, fire, water, air and ether?"

Ailwin responded, "Nue', there is a Form for everything in creation. Only a Celestine Formorian can wield all Forms. Many wizards can wield the Forms of nature but to wield all Forms there can be no separation of the inside and outside. Few wizards can hold that state of the Formless in order to wield all Forms."

"What allows a wizard to hold no separation?" I inquired.

He answered quickly, "Stillness."

Stillness was not my talent. I thought Ailwin should have chosen Thomas over me. Thomas was always still. I had not spoken aloud but Ailwin looked at me and said, "Thomas was never still despite his apparent calm demeanor. He always worried about you and your aunt. He always fretted that he needed to be the person everyone expected him to be; the protector, the provider, the father. You perceive the blue light. You remember. You do not care to be an expectation. You see. Your impatience can be harnessed."

My immediate internal response was that it was now exceedingly clear that Ailwin knew my thoughts and my incompetence would be found out. I felt naked, stripped of my façade. Despite his encouragement I felt lonely and vulnerable. Ailwin smiled at me.

By the end of the second week winter had closed in and the peaks were covered in snow. Over the following months my abilities to be still and wield the Forms matured. At the end of the third month of my training, instead of going outside and practicing, Ailwin remained in his chair at the breakfast table. Soon Pargus arrived and Ailwin instructed me to go with him. Ailwin handed me a large pack with food and supplies. It was clear this would be an extensive journey. Pargus and I set off in the cold, journeying through the Valley of the White Deer, heading into the Glacier Mountains.

I was becoming accustomed to not being let in on the plan. It irritated me but even when I asked I received little response. I asked so many questions that Ailwin began to simply smile and pat me on the head keeping the answers mute. I assumed they thought it would keep me calmer if I wasn't aware of the dangers ahead.

Around me, Pargus was haughty. He saw me as insignificant, which reflected the way I viewed myself. Pargus was a Formorian. He came from a noble family. I was uncultivated. I did what he instructed.

As Pargus and I set off, I immediately began to miss Ailwin and felt hesitation journeying into the unknown with a wolf-man. Pargus stepped with sullen determination. He seemed to be weighed down with the heaviness of an outcome.

His first instruction to me was to remain silent if we encountered any clerics. He was to be the one who handled the priests and their agents. They church had many spies who made constant inquiries. Sometimes those without the correct answers disappeared.

We had reached the base of an enormous glacier. I had never seen one before. We watched as a massive chunk fell from its leading edge, calving into the lake below. It created a thunder that racked my entire body. There was an eerie lack of life here; no trees, no grass, no birds, no deer. Blue streaks ran through the ice like internal streams. It was a land I could not have even imagined. We climbed over the most treacherous ice with precarious footings for almost a full day before we reached a high lake shore and rested. My head throbbed from the exertion and altitude. My shoe leather was cut and my hands were bleeding from a day of grasping onto ice shards.

We camped on the shore and that night my dreams were consumed with tales of insufficiency and fear. I was grateful for morning's arrival and I awoke on the frozen, hard ground with pain and stiffness coursing through my left shoulder and hip. Steam escaped my mouth and nose as my warm breath collided with the freezing air. The sky appeared as if it had been set on fire. After a hearty breakfast that consumed the last of our provisions, we headed around the left side of the lake and up a ridge. Just before midday we reached the summit. I looked onto the valley below and gasped. It was a magical place. Deer roamed freely. Flocks of yellow butterbirds flittered from tree to tree. A road lay before us leading through a green valley and into a city. The warming air was most welcome. I asked Pargus, "What is this land? Why have we come here? Why have you brought me?" He responded, "Would you please stop talking."

As we entered the valley several hundred two story buildings lined the north side of the road. It was a beehive of activity, bustling with negotiations. The structures were evenly sited with generous access. Every building's shape was uniquely irregular and each was sheathed in brown wooden shingles. All the buildings had second stories much larger than their first stories, with large overhangs making them appear unstable. Many had boxy, seemingly unsupported add-ons to the second story structure attached by only one wall They hung precariously out in space. Some buildings leaned to the right, some to the left. It was all intentional. Every detail was a statement. These were strong structures reinforced by massive silver oak beams. Every window was singularly shaped as an ode to each resident's uniqueness. The wavy glass panes were octagons, heptagons, hexagons, triangles, squares, pentagons and stars. This was the zone of commerce. Residents lived on the top floor and conducted business in their store on the bottom floor. Every time a few more children were born a new room was constructed jutting out of the existing second story. The bottom floor stores were arranged neatly so all visitors and residents could inspect and purchase wares.

The south side of the road held the orchards, perfectly aligned, stretching endlessly toward the horizon. Only the winding Ellorian river interrupted the perfect symmetrical rows. Every tree held fruits or nuts; apples, plums, pears, cherries, sorbs, quinces, apricots, walnuts, hazelnuts, almonds and chestnuts. Besides the sheer abundance and beauty, what was truly intriguing was that I was gazing upon a bucolic scene that should have only been possible at the end of summer. It was only the first days of spring. Clearly nature's patterns were being manipulated to allow the thousands of residents to thrive.

We were still three thousand yards from the city gates. As we approached, barrier rich farmland filled both sides of the valley. Great squares of vegetables and grains filled in the patchwork grid; artichokes, broad beans, chard, carrots, field peas, pumpkins, tomatoes, cardoons and cabbages. Rivet wheat, rye, barley and oat fields spread out far to the east. Food was bountiful. This was the main sustenance for a city of over one hundred and twenty-four thousand residents. My village of Chester Shire held nearly five hundred people and that seemed enormous. Elloria was not a village but a nation. It was a thriving paradise woven in a spell. As we approached the city gates, great silver oaks lined the street.

Even though we were barely emerging from the throws of winter, there was no cold here. Flowers bloomed and the air was fragranced with honeysuckle. My mood shifted from grim to elation. My curiosity was peaked and my heart was beating with eager anticipation.

I asked Pargus, "Who holds the greatest power here, the church or the royals?"

Pargus answered, "In Elloria the church is ruled by Cardinal

Gregory. He comes from a powerful family and is being groomed to be pope. His family's wealth may assure that outcome one day. He is intelligent and wields his authority subtly, allowing secular rule to remain within the royal lineage. The people support the queen when it comes to matters of this life but they follow the Cardinal when it comes to matters of the after-life."

Dominating the entrance to the city was the Basilica of Martyrs. It was the center for church activity in the northern Earthlands. Here was the power center where the shepherds could impress and rule their sheep. This was the home of Gregory the blessed.

Pargus continued, "Gregory's father had procured the title for his son two years before, at the age of 21. On his own, Gregory had added 'the blessed' to his name. Despite his youth, the Cardinal is an expert at maintaining submission to orthodoxy and dogma. Cardinal Gregory appreciates that the House of Elloria and its current ruler Alicia the first have little interest in expanding their power or wealth. Power and wealth are what matter most to Cardinal Gregory allowing an uneasy balance to be maintained between church and state."

Perched on the far end of the valley, positioned to the right of a waterfall, was the castle of Elloria. Nothing could have appeared more welcoming. Pargus looked down at me and his face alighted with a huge smile. He felt the same. I smiled because I anticipated a bath, hot food and a warm bed. Pargus smiled because he anticipated seeing Lady Alicia.

As we approached the castle it became apparent that its walls were not made of stone or wood shingles. It seemed to be blue glass but as we reached the entrance bridge I could see the castle was made of Celestine. The entire exterior of the castle was sheathed in Celestine. This crystal is more precious than emerald or gold. To see it used in such a conspicuous, copious way was beyond my imagining. Every inch of the cladding luminesced. It reminded me of the light that surrounded Ailwin.

The people who greeted us obviously knew and respected Pargus.

He had been a frequent visitor to Lady Alicia. We were escorted into the great hall. The guard told Pargus, "Lady Alicia awaits your presence."

Banners woven with golden thread hung on the walls and great ancestral statues lined the entrance walkway. But all I cared about was that I was finally warm, though oddly the room was lacking a fireplace. I expected to meet a great and delicate queen, a lady of fragile beauty clothed in gossamer silks, gold and gems. What sat before us was a warrior princess clothed in strips of alternating black and spotted dragon leather. She was a combatant ready to engage any enemy that threatened her kingdom. She was at once both beautiful and powerful, seated upon a golden throne of reverence.

Lady Alicia, as first born, had ascended to the throne five years earlier, upon her father's death. In Elloria there was no hierarchy based upon sex. Her younger brother Modren stood as the first in line should anything befall Alicia.

Pargus led me closer and when we stopped he bowed to the Lady. He gently pulled me forward and said, "My Lady, may I present Simon Baker. Simon, may I present the Lady Alicia."

I bowed, mimicking Pargus. She was intimidating. She stared at me intently, inspecting me. I was an unknown commodity. Ailwin had chosen me and all the others were required to accept his choice.

Alicia smiled and began, "Ailwin has sent you and we are pleased you have come. Over the next two months you will train with Pargus and my brother, Prince Modren. Then a company will be formed. Pargus and you should rest, eat and wash. Then I will show you the strontium mines." With a slight nod, we were dismissed.

As Pargus and I withdrew from her presence I asked him, "Pargus, what are these mines?"

He unexpectedly answered, "They hold the celestine which has made this land rich. For lifetimes, these mines have been coveted by the greedy and those seeking power. The celestine may be beautiful and cover the temples and palaces, but it can also be made into celestine diamonds. Many sorcerers and rulers have lost their lives trying to possess these mines."

That afternoon Lady Alicia led us beneath the waterfall and into the strontium mines. Gnomes and humans smiled and bowed to her as we passed on our descent. Suddenly sheer cliffs rose above us on three sides. The center opened to the sun. The cliffs were pure Celestine with natural inclusions every foot. The gnomes and humans mined the mineral with surgical precision by simply hammering on each inclusion with their wood splitters. It was now clear how the castle of Elloria had been constructed.

These mines were deep and hot and I felt claustrophobic. I was filled with a morbid fear that I had experienced many times, even before my birth. Despite the fact that I was always eager to explore I was glad to be heading out of these depths. When we returned to the castle, Alicia's brother, Prince Modren was waiting for us. He was a towering man, muscular, handsome and powerful. Being thin and slight I hesitated to approach him feeling intimidated. But he held out his hand in greeting and I was required to oblige. Modren was Alicia's only sibling. He was a prince, a famous archer and had a reputation with women and taverns. Modren was a fierce protector of Alicia and the House of Elloria.

I was a slight, inexperienced boy, cast into some unexplained intrigue. I did not understand my role, my value or my fate. Despite my love of new undertakings, this escapade was real. It was not a fantasy concocted in my imagination on a leisurely walk. It was no dream I could simply awaken from. This was a serious play where blood could be spilled, rulers overthrown and people's lives made tumultuous.

Throughout the spring, from sunup to sundown, I trained with Pargus the grey and Modren. Pargus instructed me in the Forms and Modren instructed me in the use of the bow and arrow, swords and practical means of survival. Modren and I became comrades. Modren required that I attend church every Sunday. As royalty, he knew the importance of acknowledging the importance of the papacy. He seemed reluctant to acknowledge its supremacy.

Pargus's approach to wielding the Forms was quite different than Ailwin's. He was results oriented. Pargus was attached to the outcome. He cared less about the pathway there. Ailwin had always been about shifting my inner state first and in that stillness inserting an intention, eliciting a response. Pargus's approach was to will effects.

Modren took me aside one afternoon as we were about to begin our work with the bow. He instructed me to sit. He began, "Drakantos is breeding her army. Her offspring will emerge this summer. Ussyro dragonettes are not born with fire in their belly nor are they able to fly as infants. To fly they must be one month old and to breathe fire they must reach maturity in the sixth month. Only after that can they be considered adult Ussyro dragons. Ussyro are easily influenced. It is during the first two weeks that they imprint and with this bond they come under the influence of their master. After two weeks of imprinting, it is very difficult to alter an imprint. Only a dragon whisperer can alter the first stages of imprints. When we leave the land of Elloria our mission is to discover who has imprinted with Drakantos, assess their purpose and observe if they are building an army."

As the end of my training approached I was called into the Ellorian Hall. Pargus, Modren, Lady Alicia, and a gnome named Gamny were present. Lady Alicia spoke first. "Spring is maturing in the outside world. The Ussyros are beginning to stir. The gnomes have reported that Drakantos was spied flying. It is time to discover the name of her master and their plan. Simon, you are now ready to take your place. Are you prepared and willing to enter this company?"

"My Lady," I responded. "My family is next in line to fall to this ill fate. I am honored to join this company."

She nodded and gave us final instructions. "My three Ellorian Guards and Gamny will accompany you."

Alicia continued, "The company of seven will proceed to the southeast through the land of bogs and uncover the dragon breeding grounds. The gnomes have reported that there are still humans alive in that area. Feed them and inquire if they know who Drakantos has imprinted with. I will continue to train the Ellorian dragon slayers in your absence. I have sent for Alyos, the dragon whisperer, and he is expected to arrive before you return." She rose from the throne of reverence and walked from the great hall. It was late. We would have one last comfortable night's sleep before our journey began.

Chapter Three

That night I was restless. I missed Thomas and Aunt Claire. I very much missed Ailwin. I wondered why he was not included in our company. I felt inferior, a mere child. Compared to Pargus and Modren I was truly a nue'. Now we were dispatched to be spies and reveal plots. I still did not fully understand my role. I was neither a sleuth nor a blue Formorian. But I appeared to be chosen, selected to wipe out a scourge.

As we set out that morning for the bogs I asked Pargus, "Why is Ailwin not with us?"

He answered, "Ailwin is a blue seer, a Celestine Wizard. He sees from now to the end, but as his purpose is to restore Balance, he sees all participants as one. We see good and evil. We see right and wrong. Ailwin sees life and Essence. He never reveals all that he sees. Ailwin will only intercede if the Balance remains disturbed. He believes you possess this incipient power to see. That is why you have been included in this adventure."

Pargus continued, "Ailwin, myself and Alicia once battled the Ussyro when the dragons first set their eyes on Elloria, threatening humans and gnomes. We quickly ended the Ussyro incursion before anyone was harmed. Since then, the Ussyro have kept their distance from Elloria. But now, without warning, the pestis has wiped out four villages and two mining towns and the dragons are breeding an army. The Ussyro are not clever beasts. This could not be unfolding without an imprinter. Ailwin sees where this is leading and is bringing together the forces to return the Balance. It was his hope to do this through influence, through alliances, through wielding the

Forms and through altering imprints. His hope is that the company will prevent a great war."

On the second day we had reached the bog. It was wet with alternating small ponds and blond patches of peat. There was a mossy, acrid smell in the humid air. It made my nose itch. This was a spongy land filled with insects and small birds darting every which-way snatching up endless meals. It was a land I hoped would be quickly traversed and left behind. While the birds ate the insects, the insects ate us. Gamny the gnome prepared lunch. He spoke to each insect as they landed on him appealing to each one to leave his blood intact. He never hurt one of them. I swatted the nuisances. After we had eaten, and been eaten, we set off hoping to exit this land.

It felt reassuring that Gamny was in our company. He was a gentle soul who respected life. While he was only twenty-one, he had served Alicia since his sixteenth name day. I related to him because he kept to himself and seldom revealed much of himself to others. Gamny was always clement. I often wondered what he was thinking as he quietly went about his work, making our lives better. I was never sure what he was; a saint, a servant or a holder of secrets.

By day three we arrived at the shore of Mirror Lake. Mountains, now cleared of winter snows, rimmed its northern shore. Still water spread out motionless, reflecting the mountains on its surface. There was a silence in this place and the only movement was a billowing cloud passing high above, mirrored in the still meltwater. Strangely there were no birds and, to my relief, no insects.

Two long boats were waiting for us and we turned from land to lake. The three Ellorian Guards, Baskor, Hugh and Thane, took full charge of the boats. The three were bothers. Baskor was the eldest and had been made Primus of the Ellorian Guard by Alicia. Hugh and Thane were twins and were closely bonded. Baskor had always been the more serious and responsible of the three. He assumed the role of defender while the twins were more playful and carefree. No matter their personality differences, the three were first and foremost the elite of the Ellorian Guard.

Baskor addressed us, "Hugh and Thane will row one long boat while Modren and I will row the other. Stay low and remain silent."

No one ever questioned Baskor. His word was law. Baskor protected Modren and Alicia but it was obvious to me that he maintained a respectful distance from Pargus. Baskor felt a deep allegiance to the royals.

Baskor the Primus and Alicia were the same age and had been educated by the same tutors. Growing up they had always confided in each other and held each other's secrets. In their late teens Baskor, possessing no royal blood, had the audacity to kiss Alicia. She responded with neutrality and he withdrew. The next day she explained that it was the sheer unexpectedness of the act that caused her reaction and not repulsion, status or judgment. It all felt uncomfortable and neither pursued that path. They remained confidants and maintained each other's deepest respect. Baskor held more than respect for Alicia.

Alicia's father had always made it clear that her marriage would be arranged and that her state obligations preceded love. While this was deeply engrained in her she longed for the freedom to explore the feelings she had for Baskor. He was physically strong, handsome and powerful. His Ellorian Guardsmen held him in the highest honor. He commanded them with intelligence and fairness. His progenitors were not royal but, for many Ellorian citizens, he was regarded as the second highest authority in Elloria, even above Prince Modren.

As we approached the far shore and the end of a queasy day Baskor shouted for both boats to halt before we reached the shore. A few three-foot long sea snakes wound their way across the water's surface. There should have been many fishing boats from the village but there were none, only snakes hissing at us. Baskor shouted a terse order, "Something is wrong. Row quickly to the south shore."

Within minutes the number of snakes grew to the point where they were nearly a solid mass slithering over one another on the water's surface. Their numbers continued to build and they piled one upon the other until several slipped into the boat itself. Modren grabbed two in one hand and threw them back. But the snakes were too numerous to throw out one or two at a time and within seconds the bottom of the boats were filled with serpents slithering over our feet and legs, leaving a glossy slime in their wake. Their fangs were reaching for any bare flesh they could find exposed. Hugh yelled, "They are poisonous. Do not let them find skin." Everyone was tossing them overboard but their numbers were gaining. Hundreds more were approaching the boats. Baskor turned toward Pargus and yelled, "Do something Pargus."

Pargus hesitated. He looked at Baskor but remained unmoving. I closed my eyes as a snake coiled up my leg and wrapped around my waist. I spoke, "Angius Somnum."

The snakes stopped moving and fell to the bottom of the boat. Pargus instructed us to throw them overboard. The snakes in the lake floated on the surface, unmoving. We rowed quickly to shore and disembarked. Baskor asked me what I had done. I said, "I allowed the Form of Sopor to penetrate the snakes. I put them to sleep. The Forms will support life more fiercely than death so we must work with their preferences. The Forms are generally creative, not destructive."

I turned toward Pargus, "Could you have shapeshifted into a snake eating creature?"

Pargus laughed and said, "The grey wolf is my animal guide. Over the years I have become him and he has become me so we are able to shift. You assumed I was a shapeshifter but I am a Grey Formorian who has merged with his Acharya animal. I do not like snakes and hesitated. My apologies. Thank you for your assistance."

Outwardly I accepted his excuse and apology. Inwardly I did not appreciate being forced to make a snap decision to take control. I bristled at being put in a situation where my ability to wield the Forms was tested and lives hung in the balance. It might have turned out badly.

Baskor told the company that this had been a thriving fishing village when he visited the year before. It now appeared abandoned except for the vulgoyles that circled above and lingered near corpses, picking at dead remains. "We will head toward the southeast now and find the breeding grounds of the Ussyro."

Upon reaching shore we disembarked and walked through a flock of twenty vulgoils who were hopping around the remains of long dead humans and gnomes, inspecting bones to see if any meat had been overlooked. Vulgoils always disconcerted me. Their ghoulish, elongated, bald faces, red necks and razor sharp, hooked beaks made for ripping flesh were intimidating. Their hair covered ears, menacingly pulled back in permanent attack mode, were the exact image of the vulgoil rainspouts on church cathedrals that made us all fearful of hell. With their exceptional eyesight they watched us closely, protecting their carrion. Their bodies were large and thickly covered with feathers, in contrast to their bald necks and faces. They had been obviously well fed. We made camp for the night as it was clear exhaustion was setting in.

Gamny the gnome cooked with great care to the delight of the entire company. Despite his own fatigue he heated water for us to wash ourselves and prepared a hearty meal of barley soup, cheese, bread and nuts. After dinner Baskor and his brother Hugh explored the surrounding caves. When they returned, they conversed with their brother Thane. I was excluded from their conversation. Soon everyone retired and finally we slept.

The next day they led us to a low promontory that overlooked a great plain. As we stared out onto the vast open landscape we could see it was dotted with small circles, over one thousand ellipses carefully spaced two feet apart. As I focused on the one closest I could see that these were nests built of small stones, each with an embryo placed in the center. There was a perceptible movement coming from inside the embryo and through its semi-transparent casing I could see the infant dragon inside.

Baskor coldly observed, "There must be a thousand embryos in this one field. If four villages were destroyed there could be an army of four thousand dragons being bred. We must find out if there are any humans remaining. We will search the caves."

In the third cave a single family was discovered; a father, mother and two teenage boys. The father was named Johannes. He was rather heavyset, which was not the norm and seemed overly educated for a fisherman. In most villages there is only enough food to maintain life and formal education is only available in the monasteries. He related his family's story to the whole company as we shared food with them. "Last fall three strangers had appeared in the village. These men were not from this area and wore capeline hats and red quilted doublets covered by paltock jackets. They remained for only three days, reticent to interact. The evening after they departed fleas were everywhere and by the end of the week the pestis had broken out.

I saw them place one snake in the estuary before they left. As soon as that snake entered the water the reptile molted, ripping its skin near its mouth and shedding its cutis. Two snakes emerged from the old scale covering.

Within four days people were coming down with fever. Many were vomiting and blood was oozing from their mouths and noses. The skin on their fingers, toes and noses turned black. The doctor bled the people and only hurried their death along. When I saw the first cases I brought my family to the caves. To my knowledge we are the only ones who survived. My sons and I fish the stream at night. We do not go out in the daytime because that is when the Drakina Dragon flies and places her embryos."

Baskor asked him if the dragon had grey horns on the back of her neck. He replied, "Yes. It appears she had three but only two remain. One has been cut out."

Baskor said, "That is Drakantos. She is the Drakina, the mother of the Ussyro dragons. Do you know with whom she has imprinted?"

Johannes did not understand and Baskor asked in another way. "Do you know her master?"

Johannes answered, "Several weeks ago two men passed by the caves and we offered them fish. They were from one of the western villages that had been ravaged by the black scourge. They were

36

searching for a place to settle but had only seen depredation. They said only one person could be responsible for this; Kalshor Dax. As soon as Kalshor installed himself as the dynast of Themos, the pestis arrived. The eastern Earthlands were decimated. The Drakina arrived and the fields were turned into hatcheries."

Baskor told us, "Prepare to leave immediately. He turned toward the family and said, "You may come if you wish. We return to Elloria."

The mother told Baskor, "You must wait until it is dark or the Drakina will spot you."

Baskor knew that with so many people now in the cave any dragon could smell the company. He was curious how four people had escaped Drakantos's olfactory prowess for so long. He said, "There is no time to waste. We leave now."

We departed the cave. The sun was bright and clouds dotted the sky. As we approached the base of the hill the shadow of Drakantos flying above momentarily blocked the sun as she observed her next kill. Baskor yelled. "Run for the boats."

But it was too late. She had eyed her prey and there was no mistaking her intention. Fear gripped me. I had never seen a real dragon before, lest one with her ears pulled back in attack mode trying to kill me. Drakantos was an exceptional specimen and she was protecting her progeny. Her inflight maneuvers made it clear she had spotted us and you could hear the low growl she produced deep within her chest. Under my breath, I whispered, "doomed" as I ran.

She swooped down, her haunches leading forward. With her left leg claw, she tore into the shoulder of the eldest son. He gasped but continued to run. Drakantos circled higher preparing for another onslaught. I waited for her to pass under the asperitas cloud and chanted, "Caelum Fulgor."

A blinding bolt of lightning shot from the cloud and struck Drakantos in the left knee burning deeply into the crus of her leg. Her screech was so shrill and the thunder clasp so powerful that we were shaken as the sounds pierced our ears. She abandoned her quarry and flew off. Only the smell of rank, burnt scales remained. The entire company was filled with frisson and no one was interested in seeing if the Drakina would return. We did not look back and soon boarded the boats. This time the serpents kept their distance. The mother tended to her son's wounds. We all headed home to Elloria.

Chapter Four

Several days later eleven of us entered the city gates. Alicia led the greeting party. She remarked, "The company has multiplied."

The next day the company of seven and Johannes met to develop clarity around the plot Kalshor Dax was hatching. Johannes had asked Baskor if he could join the company. He addressed Baskor with great respect and gratitude. "You have saved my family. I owe you our lives. I know the lands to the east all the way to the Port of Themos. I could be invaluable to your party as a pathfinder." Baskor nodded in the affirmative and then asked the party, "What is Kalshor's objective?"

Hugh chimed in, "And why did he begin in the Port of Themos?"

There was a pause. In the stillness a familiar soft blue light filled the doorway and Ailwin entered. My heart rejoiced as I jumped to my feet to greet him. To his left was Alyos, the dragon whisperer. Everyone except Johannes rose in respect and bowed. Johannes apparently had no idea who these people were. Baskor grabbed his arm and raised him to standing position. As Alyos move away from Ailwin and seated himself I could see that the blue light also surrounded Alyos.

After greetings, we settled in. Ailwin spoke first. "Hugh's question is important. Alyos, what is near the Port of Themos that is most valuable?"

Alyos answered, "There are the jewels of the Lady of Themos and there is the Bliokasha, the library of the ancients. Directly to the west of Themos are the two gold mines of Themos."

Ailwin prodded him further, "And what does The Bliokasha hold that would be of the greatest value to someone like Kalshor Dax?"

Alyos said, "The repository holds the spells of the ancients in its deepest vaults."

Ailwin nodded and elaborated, "Kalshor Dax cannot wield the Forms. The resistance he has faced from the Formorians and his family's disgrace have gnawed away at him until his mind has become dark with hate. This hatred is what we are seeing unfold now. Though it is forbidden even to the blue Formorians, the Bliokasha contains one formula that would allow Kalshor Dax his revenge; the Elixir of Sanitat. He could control a power woven from the threads of Essence. He could manipulate the Essence of death itself. Kalshor Dax could rule an army of immortals and he could become immortal. We must assume that since he controls the library of the ancients he now has the formula in his possession.

Once one starts to imbibe the elixir one is required to drink the tincture on a regular basis to maintain immortality. He who drinks the tincture pays a cost for this imbibing. Kalshor Dax will appear as an enchanter, a protector and one who bestows wealth to those who follow him. But they will never be told the payment he exacts from them.

Sanitat is brewed with:
   5 pinches of gold Essence
   4 drops of dragon horn blood
   2 pinches of Celestine blue diamond dust
   9 drops of sea snake venom
   2 grains of silver oak.

One is required to swallow only five drops of the mixture but there is a great irony. Some do not survive the internal agony generated by the potion as it morphs the body into its state of immutability. And this process must be repeated every three days as the effects are temporary. That which gives you invincibility, immutability and immortality can kill you if the source is withdrawn."

Ailwin continued, "To the west of the Port of Themos, near the gold mines, a massive smelter has been constructed to process the gold ore. The humans and gnomes that survived the pestis have been enslaved to work the mines and smelter. Gold Essence requires countless refinements but Kalshor Dax is well on his way to creating gold Essence.

The Ussyro dragons are the only breed with dragon horns on their necks. He is not breeding an army. He is breeding dragon horn blood. Drakantos thinks his imprinter is building an Ussyro army to rule the humans, but Kalshor Dax will slaughter the Drakina's brood when the time comes.

As your company discovered, the waters of the fishing villages have been infested with sea snakes assuring a steady supply of venom. That leaves only two ingredients he must acquire; Celestine diamonds and silver oak. Alyos continues to protect the land of Elloria with the Form of Aegis so we believe the city, the Celestine and the silver oaks are secure."

In all the Earthlands there were only two blue Formorians and both Ailwin and Alyos were sitting at our table. Alyos rose to speak. He was imposing. He looked only thirty years of age and his hair was long, silky and golden. He was very tall and there were no wrinkles on his hairless face. The back of his left hand held a deep scar from a dragon's claw. "The land of Elloria contains the only ore deposits of Celestine. Celestine diamonds are harvested by submerging blocks in dragon acid. The acid eats away the mineral allowing the diamonds of blue light to remain. Because both the silver oaks and Celestine lie within the boundaries of Elloria it is probable Kalshor will set his sights on this land."

Modren rose. "Kalshor Dax will not enter our gates as long as I remain alive. We must interrupt his plan at every point. We must attack the smelter and destroy the embryos."

His sister rose, gently put her hand on his shoulder and allowed him to be seated. "Kalshor Dax comes from an Ellorian bloodline. His grandfather was in the Ellorian Guard. His grandfather was banished for treachery and a failed attempt to become Ellorian Primus. He was labeled a traitor and cast out of Elloria. This hatred has been brewing for generations.

The gnomes report that there are many humans wandering among the four villages. They are barely surviving. Thousands more will die if we do not offer our help. I have ordered the mining here to cease. The entrance to the mine has been sealed and the storeroom of Celestine diamonds has been locked. The human and gnome miners will be tasked with sending food to the ravaged villages. Ours must be a clandestine operation for Kalshor Dax and Drakantos must not be aware we have detected their plot. Our first priority must be to stabilize the population. We will open our gates to refugees."

Pargus objected, "Refugees are a threat. They may have pestis. These migrants will strain our resources. They may be in league with Kalshor Dax. We have no way of knowing who is friend and who is foe. Their ranks are infiltrated with addicts, drug dealers, rapists and murderers. Cardinal Gregory will not appreciate filling the city with poor that will require charity."

Lady Alicia retorted, "I understand your comments come from the love in your heart to protect the people of Elloria. We will allow refugees to settle in the fields to the west of the gates and supply them with what is needed to farm and raise animals. We will offer them each a small bocland to farm, clothing, food and hope."

She continued, "We will lead the army of dragon slayers south, staying to the north of the devastated villages and make camp north of the gold mines. Kalshor Dax is reported to be building barriers around the port of Themos. If we cannot enter Themos we will attempt to deny him his supply of gold."

Ailwin stood and walked to the head of the table. "Alyos and I have work to do and will leave at sunrise. The embryos will not hatch for another month so Kalshor Dax cannot act now. We have time on our side. Simon will come with us. The three Ellorian Guards will lead the army and create a camp north of the gold mines. Gamny will accompany them. The Lady Alicia, Modren, Johannes and Pargus will remain here and build defenses for the city. If the Land of Elloria falls, Kalshor Dax will rule all the Earthlands. Pargus will strengthen the Forms that guard the city. Alyos, Simon and I will return before the hatching of the embryos occurs."

With that the congregation split into three companies. In the morning the company of Formorians comprising Ailwin, Alyos and myself set off to the west. As far as I was concerned my time of being a nue' was over.

Chapter Five

Over the next week we retraced our steps and returned over the Glacier Mountains, through the Valley of the White Deer and into the Forest of Red Oaks. Ailwin informed us, "I have called the Council of Formorians. The other two will arrive at the Circle of Irminsul in two days. As Pargus has remained in Elloria, Simon, you will take his place."

I asked Ailwin, "There are a total of six Formorians; yourself, Alyos, Pargus, the two sisters and myself?"

He answered with a smile, "So you consider yourself to be one of us now? So be it. It has been your destiny. You have embraced it and so you will join us. You may not be a nue' anymore but there is still wisdom to gain and skill to acquire." I nodded and inwardly rejoiced.

Two days later, Ailwin, Alyos the dragon whisperer and I arrived at the Circle of Irminsul. As we approached we saw that the two Formorians sisters had already arrived. They were ancient and generally spent their days in silence immersed in the Formless. They were rarely involved in human matters. The taller one was considered an oracle.

There was no joy in our greeting. Everyone stood and stared. The seven ancient silver oaks were gone. The impact of what we were witnessing shook us. No one could speak. Only the freshly chopped stumps remained. Splinters covered the earth. A path of destruction led into the woods where the precious silver oaks had been dragged away.

We remained one step behind Kalshor Dax. I could feel a despondency enter my heart. We needed to report this to the others in Elloria and were preparing to depart when the sister arose. Her eyes glassed over and she spoke strange words;

> In the time of trials, the circle will fall
> The deceiver will enter, and the devils will call
> The Essence will shudder, defiled by the pawn
> The truth will be twisted, protection withdrawn
> The beasts will be banished from history's story
> The Balance will tarnish, bereft of its glory

Chapter Six

The Port of Themos was a merchant city. It held the enviable position of being the largest and deepest harbor on the east coast. The commerce fair was a permanent centerpiece of the town. Mercantilism was dominated by the gnomes. The city's ruler controlled the trade licenses and thus controlled which ships could enter the port. Every shipper paid the ruler a carnage fee to load and unload their ship. The ruler also controlled the cheminage travel tolls and through them wielded the power of access. The ruler held firm control and made sure the town was meticulously maintained. Hucksters were routinely rounded up and every aspect of trade was vigilantly protected. All merchants were required to pay their taxes. Bribes were illegal but were not unheard of. Textiles, wine, Christian relics, weapons, gold, leather, spices and food stuffs filled the city warehouses. There were several merchants that dealt in horses, pigs and cattle.

Themos was the center of church power. The papal estates lined the northeast coast of Themos separated by tall stone walls from the main city. Here the pope and his cardinals prayed for us sinners and made the decisions how to collect more wealth and how to spend it on themselves. When the pestis arose, the entire cadre of church officials left for their estates in the countryside and waited out the epidemic. I assumed they were offering prayers for the starving and dead. The church sent no aid and left the corpses to the vulgoils.

Kalshor Dax and two generations of relatives before him had lived in exile in the far eastern seaport of Tres. As a young man he had worked on the ships that made regular trips to Themos to trade. He saw the wealth, the prosperity and the way the people of Themos thrived and it made his blood boil with hatred. He had only known a disgraced family name, poverty and neglect. His father repeated one message to him on a daily basis, "You are a good for nothing." Kalshor Dax wanted his revenge. He wanted dominion over the western Earthlands and it was a plan motivated by anger and insufficiency. It was not power or wealth that drove him. He wanted the people who had turned his family into pariahs to suffer as he had suffered. He wanted them either enslaved or dead.

Kalshor's relationship with the church was one of convenience. He would pay large sums of tribute to the church as long as it remained unobstructive to his plans and rule. Non-interference and inaction could be bought.

He had made a compact with Emrich Chuzo, the owner of the shipping line for which he worked. Together they would seize the Port of Themos and control the trade routes encompassing all the eastern shipping lanes. Emrich was already rich but the thought of controlling Themos and the four other midland seaports was too tempting. Kalshor had seduced him with his simple plan. Together they conscripted six hundred fair-haired Huntsmen from the Bitterlands of the northeast. They lured them with the promise of gold and adventure.

Themos was not a military base. It was a commercial powerhouse and only lightly defended. City workers were not militia but tax collectors. Hidden by the darkness of night, in the quiet of the predawn hours, six ships carrying the six hundred Huntsmen mercenaries landed in the Port of Themos and disembarked. They split into six contingents securing the port, the commerce district, the city's major entrances and exits and the government nerve centers. The ruler, the port authorities and the few guardsmen were caught unprepared for the tactical suppression of the entire city and within a single day the city had fallen.

The Huntsmen were opportunists. They saw women, children, men and animals as expendable obstacles to procuring gold. They were an amoral race who enjoyed drinking, debauchery and adventure. They were willing to take risks.

The merchants of the city did not want to die so they allowed the Huntsmen to take the city in the hope that the merchants would be allowed to trade and prosper. The Themos merchants cared only about wealth and survival, not political power.

After the city had been secured, Kalshor Dax, along with Emrich Chuzo and his family, settled in Themos. One evening Kalshor Dax and the six hundred Huntsmen disappeared, replaced by a mass of bloodsucking fleas that infested Themos with pestis. Within a month the city was decimated. No other ships would go near the city as the pestis meant certain death. No armies would rescue the great port from her fate. Emrich and his family were the only ones buried in separate graves. Months later, the fleas had died and Kalshor and the Huntsmen moved back in and captured the gold mines to the west. In a repeat of Themos's fate, the four other villages west of Themos fell to waves of fleas. With the gold secured, Kalshor Dax imported six thousand more Huntsmen.

Kalshor Dax had stripped the four villages of food to sustain the Huntsmen who were now Kalshor's chosen race. The warehouses of Themos were laid bare for the benefit of the Huntsmen. If materials were insufficient, ships were sent to outlying ports to be pillaged. Four other seaports were seized. The Huntsmen became both loyal and dependent.

Kalshor wanted every inch of Elloria burned, its great orchards and abundant fields blackened, its people enslaved. Above all else, he wanted Modren and Alicia dead. His vision was to end the lineage of The House of Elloria. He wanted it wiped off the map, removed from history. Kalshor Dax would replace it with his own lineage and history. His reign would begin with his rule of Themos but he envisioned his revenge extending throughout all the Earthlands.

Kalshor had signed a treaty of non-interference with the pope. As long as Kalshor tithed one tenth of Themos's wealth to the church, the church would allow Kalshor to rule. Should the payments end, the pope would assure that Kalshor's dominion would end.

Chapter Seven

The three brothers, Baskor, Hugh and Thane led the Ellorian Guard and an army of ten thousand dragon slayers toward Themos. With great stealth they passed through the lands east of Mirror Lake and north of the gold mines. Here they set up an encampment.

While the Primus and his brothers moved the army east, Alicia, her brother Modren, Pargus the grey and Johannes settled refugees, secured the city and brought some sense of stability to the countryside. The guild of commerce had protested the location of the new settlement so near the merchant center but the shop owners soon rejoiced at the steady wave of orders for goods needed to supply the refugees.

There had been no further reports of pestis. The Port of Themos, under Kalshor's rule, was quiet. Trade and shipping were flourishing once again.

Pargus and Alicia planned to join the armies as soon as the three Formorians returned. Pargus the grey had met Lady Alicia three year earlier. Pargus had been sent by Ailwin to protect the Ellorians when the dragons began massing near its northwest borders. At that time the dragon horde was poorly led and generally undisciplined. Pargus, Alicia and her force of dragon slayers had easily repelled the incursion and scattered the Ussyro weyr. Their time together had bonded them. Pargus had regularly visited Lady Alicia even though he was not of royal blood. The fact that he was a Formorian seemed to supersede that disqualification. Pargus was disdainful yet charismatic. His stunningly handsome appearance caught Lady Alicia off guard. He was a powerful Formorian and knew how to charm when necessary.

Alicia was infatuated. Beauty attracts and, for a time, conceals the flaws.

Baskor tried his best to be a perfectly professional general, always offering respect to both Pargus and Alicia. Deep down his stomach clenched and his jealousy toward Pargus smoldered.

I held Pargus at bay. He looked upon me with scorn, as a mere child usurping power. Pargus was not a blue Formorian and it seemed that there was some unexplained reason he never would be.

The company stationed in Elloria made preparations to leave at dawn for the dragon slayer's encampment. Modren was to remain in the city for its continued protection. Ailwin, Alyos and I had returned to Elloria that evening and reported to the company the fate of the Circle of Irminsul. Pargus was deeply affected by the news. His ancestors had planted the seven silver oaks many generations ago as a coven of hope that Formorian wisdom and power could prevent any more wars. The dashing of that hope created a deep sadness in him and combined with the realization that the only ingredient Kalshor needed now was Celestine, shook him to the core. He spent that evening alone, brooding.

That night Prince Modren made one last round of inspections in the castle. He walked into the humid passage under the waterfall. The first door on the left was the entrance to the mine storehouse. The seal on the massive oak doors had been broken and two guards lay dead at the exposed entrance. He walked in and immediately saw that the chest of blue Celestine diamonds was gone. He ran out of the storehouse and down the passage that exited through the mountain. Modren spotted Johannes and four other humans carrying off the chest. Johannes and two men turned to face Modren while the other two, carrying the chest of diamonds, continued to make their escape.

Modren shouted at Johannes, "What is this treachery?" Modren caught the man closest to him by the neck and with a definitive crack, ended his life. Then he turned toward Johannes. "Why Johannes?"

Johannes faced him with a resistant stance, his right hand drawing his estoc sword. "When Kalshor Dax's spies entered my village, they promised to spare me and my family from the pestis if I infiltrated your city and relieved you of the diamonds. I did not know you or your people and only wanted to spare my family. Being discovered in the caves by your company gave me the opportunity I needed. If I did not deliver Kalshor's prize my family would have been killed."

Modren wrapped his cape around his arm and plunged at Johannes diverting the sword's blade. With his left hand clenched, Johannes landed a powerful blow to Modren's stomach and Modren doubled over. Modren rose slowly and drew his sword. This was no contest and Johannes knew that. Johannes turned away and tried to run but Modren grabbed him and, with a powerful blow, Modren's fist, which held the sword hilt, broke the infidel's jaw. Before Modren could turn his attention to the other man, a rock crushed into the left side of Modren's head and he fell to the ground, unconscious. The thief who wielded the blow said to Johannes, "We will take him as our insurance." Within minutes the four remaining thieves, a bound and barely conscious Modren and the Celestine blue diamonds were loaded onto a boat headed to Themos. The bodies of the two guards and the thief remained on the floor of the passageway. It was not until the next morning that the three bodies were discovered. The company was informed of the theft. We had to assume Kalshor Dax now had his five elements.

Chapter Eight

Ailwin believed there was still a chance that time was on our side and believed we should confront the Huntsmen before they had distilled the Elixir of Sanitat. Over the following days the company of Ailwin, Alyos the dragon whisperer, Pargus the grey, Alicia and myself made our way to the army's camp. We informed Baskor, Hugh and Thane of the treachery and what we might encounter. Pargus intimated that he was not totally sure Modren was a captive. Could it have been Modren who had killed the three and taken the Celestine diamonds? Of course, no other person in the company had even considered that and the suggestion was summarily dismissed.

No one had ever faced any army of invincibles. Thane suggested it was certain defeat to fight. Hugh agreed, but then Hugh always agreed with his twin. Alyos made the Formorian position clear. To attack now there was at least a chance. To retreat and wait for a direct assault on Elloria by sixty-six hundred impervious Huntsmen meant certain defeat. The Lady Alicia said her armies would engage the enemy. It was certain the rescue of Modren was part of her calculation. The decision had been made.

Alicia addressed us, "The fate of Elloria and the Earthands depend upon the months of preparations we have made. Soon this world will be filled with a new generation of dragons bred with evil and intent upon our demise. Left unchecked, the Huntsmen will tear the fabric of our lives to shreds. We must end Kalshor's malefic plan before it takes root."

Alicia ordered all ten thousand dragon slayers to go directly south and mass at Antor Cleft, the land between Themos and the two gold mines. This would divide the mines from Themos. The troops would camp just to the west of the pyramid of Myros. There were no Huntsmen working the mines so little resistance was expected from the west. The Ellorian slayers would create a pincer movement and half of the dragon slayers would move to envelop the northern half of the city and the other half would move to enfold the southern half of the city. There could be little chance of a retreat toward the sea. The Huntsmen were barracked in the city center and this move would surround Kalshor's forces. If the slayers could catch the Huntsmen unprepared and if the Sanitat was not yet formulated there was hope.

The dragon slayers had their orders. The incursion would begin at midnight. In the darkness of night, in complete silence, the forces moved into position east of the Myros pyramid near the city's western entrance. Dragon slayers are experts at moving without detection and the army was in position by the first light of dawn. Baskor, Hugh, Thane and Lady Alicia led the forces into the city easily skirting the city's unfinished defensive walls.

Kalshor's Huntsmen were caught off guard as they emerged from their barracks. Our arrows rained down upon them like a hail storm. Hundreds of arrows pierced the Huntsmen's flesh and they fell quickly to our slayers as they emerged from their barracks. But then the wounded rose back up, ripped out the arrows that had penetrated their flesh and stood their ground in defiance. Thousands of Huntsmen exited the barracks and descended upon our forces. Our spears, arrows and swords could penetrate and slow them but nothing would stop them.

Each Huntsmen held a scimitar in their right hand and a halberd axe in the other. They were powerful men wielding lethal weapons. With a single blow they were able to split open the head of a slayer, laying them waste.

Hugh pulled the arrow back in his bow and shot a Huntsman point blank through the forehead. The Huntsman stood staring at Hugh, stunned, the arrow deeply lodged in his brain. Hugh expected him to fall but the Huntsman attacked with his axe raised, the arrow seemingly ineffective. Hugh let fly another arrow into his left eye momentarily halting his forward attack. The Huntsman groaned angrily and ripped out the arrow, eye attached. Hugh watched in shock as the empty eye socket healed itself, the Sanitat generating a new eye.

Thane jumped onto the back of one Huntsman, reached around with his knife and slit his throat. The Huntsman fell to the ground blood spurting from his neck with each heartbeat. The Huntsman moaned in agony holding his throat. Within seconds the blood stopped pumping out of his neck and the gash healed. The Huntsman rose and moved toward Thane. Lady Alicia watched this as she let her arrow fly into the Huntsman. Thane turned toward Alicia and shouted above the din, "We cannot kill them. Their blood runs with Kalshor's poison."

She sounded the retreat. The Formorians had remained in the rear to the east. Running in retreat, the dragon slayers passed the Formorian position. The Huntsmen were powerfully muscled but their stout, bulky bodies made them slow in their pursuit. As the last of the slayers passed the Formorians, in unison the Formorians uttered, "Turris Vagus." Hundreds of rock spires taller than three men shot out of the ground releasing a huge cracking sound as they broke through the earth's crust separating the Huntsmen from the dragon slayers. Dust and rocks flew into the air as the massive stone shards thrust out from the earth's core. As the land shook, the rock spires encircled the Huntsmen, imprisoning them in a wall of towering rock. They wailed. Screams of frustration bellowed from their ranks. They wanted blood and there would be no more today. Alicia knew that it would only be hours before the Huntsmen found a way to escape. She ordered the troops back to Elloria.

Over two hundred dragon slayers were lost but the core of the army remained intact. They made their way back to Elloria and the wounded were attended to. Modren remained in enemy hands.

Chapter Nine

Ailwin, Alyos, Pargus and I met as soon as we returned to Elloria. Pargus addressed the company of Formorians, "Kalshor Dax has broken the code and used Sanitat. He has disordered the Essence, ripping at the fabric of life. The only way to defeat his army is to balance it with an opposing Essence. In a short time, he will mount a direct assault upon Elloria. If we encase the entire army of Huntsmen in the Form of Temporus we can move time forward three days and make the elixir impotent."

Alyos retorted, "We are also forbidden to disorder the Essence. Even to restore the Balance we are forbidden. Just because Kalshor Dax manipulates the Essence of Death it does not give us permission to manipulate the Essence of Time. You are talking about changing the fabric of time. We must not give ourselves a dispensation and absolve ourselves for disrupting the highest order of Essence. We should destroy the dragons and deprive Kalshor of one element. Drakantos was missing only one neck horn and there have been no more available to Kalshor. Removing too many horns will kill Drakantos and Kalshor will not risk that before the babies are born. I believe the reason he has not directly attacked Elloria is because he has little of the Elixir in hand. The dragon embryos will not hatch for several weeks."

Pargus responded tersely, "And we thought he had no elixir before and so we attacked, destroying the lives of hundreds of dragon slayers. The intelligence from our spies is deficient. And there are over four thousand embryos protected by an imprinted, fully mature Ussyro. These dragons are difficult to kill. As adults their only vulnerabilities are Celestine spears, suffocating them by extinguishing the fire in

55

their belly, and geant mongoose. If we can't change time then we will be attacked."

Ailwin spoke, "When we feel under threat our survival instinct rears its head and our reaction is self-preservation at any cost. We want to lash out. Then killing becomes an option. Yes, we could kill the dragons and slaughter four thousand animals, but we could also nurture the dragons and imprint with them turning an enemy into a friend. Alyos, you are a dragon whisperer. What would be required to imprint the babies?"

Alyos answered, "First we would have to deal with Drakantos, their mother. She will be protective. Dragons operate mainly through smell and sound. Imprinting would begin with acclimating the babies with our smell. Then we must fix firmly in them a dependency on us. For a dragon this occurs most deeply through feeding. Baby dragons are omnivores. They eat fruit, vegetables, insects, crickets, cockroaches, mice, rats and mealworms. Lastly there is the resonance. Dragons are especially drawn to the sounds of very low frequency growls. Love is expressed through the hissing growl Grryo Grryo Sss. Whispering to a dragon is soothing them with this purr. Together the smell, feeding and hissing create the imprint."

Ailwin asked Alyos, "There are four villages that have been turned into nesting grounds. Is it possible for one Formorian to imprint a thousand baby dragons?"

Alyos responded, "The babies will all hatch at the dawn that follows the full moon. That is in twelve days. If we position one Formorian with each brood we would be able to imprint each brood to that particular Formorian."

A plan was formulated and the company of four Formorians headed out.

Chapter Ten

D rakantos was based in the eastern-most nest that lay between Antor Cleft and Mirror Lake. Alyos was chosen to patrol that brood and their mother because of his skills as a dragon whisperer. He took up his position first. Then I was chosen for the western-most village. Pargus and Ailwin took their places in the two middle villages. Each village held a nest of nearly a thousand embryos.

I was thinking it wiser to simply destroy the embryos. They were unprotected and vulnerable. It would not be difficult to cut each one open and kill the babies. But Ailwin was adamant. He directed us. "The dragons are innocents and you are forbidden to kill them." I assumed now that killing would be a last resort. I wondered if, even then, Ailwin would allow their death.

The night of the full moon arrived. The land was eerily illuminated by the moonbeams. I was particularly unsettled and sleep was not on my agenda. I was only sixteen and unfamiliar with adventures, wars and dragons. My ability to wield the Forms was not tried and true. Here I stood, alone, in a decimated village containing a thousand pebble nests, each seeded with an Ussyro dragon bred to destroy me. And they were about to hatch.

With the first light of dawn movement within the embryos increased. The babies were clawing at their embryonic sacks in an attempt to free themselves. Each undulated with increasing motion. As the dawn's light appeared the four Formorians, solitary and unseen, each plucked one hair from their arm and spoke the words. "Mus Surrecturus."

The hair grew and morphed into a mouse and then another and

within seconds thousands of mice were scrambling everywhere. I found it quite disconcerting that each was birthed from my hair but then it was my smell and the food that was important. Each mouse was a part of me. The infants were starting to break through, their claws penetrating the embryonic casings. Then their noses emerged, sniffing wildly, frantically searching to imprint with their mother. What they found were mice. As their heads emerged they lunged at the mice voraciously swallowing them without chewing. It was pandemonium; one thousand baby Ussyro dragons ripping at their embryonic shells, freed, and pouncing upon the scattering mice. They were ravenous and wanted to be satiated.

Within minutes every dragon had hatched and every mouse had been devoured. Then I walked into the middle of the chaos and began the resonance. Over and over, I repeated Grryo Grryo Sss, Grryo Grryo Sss.

The babies could barely walk and steadied themselves with their wing tips. They were vulnerable and could not yet fly. They would not be able to breathe fire for months. They were searching now for someone to imprint with. As I repeated the resonance and whispered to them, all their faces turned toward me. One thousand babies, inched toward me. The olfactory nerves running along each side of their noses pulsated with visible throbs. They jostled and pushed over each other to be able to capture my smell. Upon recognition they surrounded me, clumsily falling as they crowded around me. I continued hissing Grryo Grryo Sss. Within minutes they were huddled against me, fed, imprinted and at peace. I felt like their mother. But then I realized this was only the beginning of the plan.

The other Formorians successfully repeated what had just transpired with my brood. Only Alyos had complications. Drakantos's maternal instincts ignited her one-pointed, matriarchal drive to imprint with her babies. She ignored the mice as the babies smelled and frantically devoured them. Alyos had to make sure she did not intermingle with them or her smell would overpower that of the mice and the plan would fail. Alyos had to maintain resonance and secure the imprint. He began to whisper Grryo Grryo Sss.

Alyos spied the wood vines growing near the Drakina's perch where she stood watching her hatchlings emerge. He spoke; "Vinea Innecto." In a flash the wood vines wrapped around the rear legs of the mother dragon and held her fast. She roared with frustration as they prevented her from entering the hatching and feeding frenzy. Then she looked at Alyos and calmed.

Alyos could hear the subtle sound of Grryo Grryo Sss emerging from the throat of Drakantos. He now stood within a few feet of her, barely out of her reach. Her hissing grew louder and louder until it was clearly audible everywhere within the hatchery. A thousand faces turned from Alyos to her. Alyos knew that with one mighty blast of fire Drakantos could burn the wood vines and free herself. Alyos spoke again; "Rostrum Convelo." The vines wrapped around her snout and sealed her mouth closed. With this, her fire and her hissing were shut down.

Alyos waded into the menagerie of babies and began to whisper Grryo Grryo Sss. All eyes were now fixed on Alyos. They smelled him and heard his resonance and the imprint held. He knew he did not have unlimited time before Drakantos freed herself. Continuing to whisper, Alyos led his brood of a thousand baby Ussyros toward Elloria while the sounds of Drakantos thrashing to free herself fell into the distant background.

In several days all the Formorians had arrived at the outskirts of Elloria with their weyr of knee-high baby Ussyro dragons. Consternation was high within the city. The refugees that had settled in the newly annexed surrounds were especially on edge wondering where four thousand dragons would stay. Would they be displaced again or would they become dragon fodder?

Lady Alicia and the Formorians met to determine the next step. Pargus congratulated the other Formorians on their accomplishment and made a bold suggestion, "Could the dragons be incorporated into the army of dragon slayers? The babies could be trained for the army."

Alyos spoke, "We must also make another determination. After two weeks, imprinting is set and cannot be altered. The baby Ussyro have been imprinted for less than one week. It would be possible in the next week to set the permanent imprint to one person instead of four. That would concentrate great power in the hands of one person but it would make handling them more cohesive."

Lady Alicia rose and addressed them, "I am afraid the dragon slayers would feel betrayed if we incorporated dragons into the army. For generations they fought the northern dragons. Now they would have to trust their lives to them. I would suggest we create four thousand nests, one set on each hill top, rock spire and peak in the mountains that boarder the city. The Ussyro should be put under one Formorian's imprint and trained to be the kingdom's protectors."

The company agreed and the city set to build the nests and provide for the dragons. Pargus was chosen to be the master imprinter. By the third month the sight of tiny dragonettes flying over the skies of Elloria became commonplace. The residents began to accept their new protectors. Mice and cockroaches were no longer a problem in the alleyways. Pargus was now the Formorian Dragon Lord. Lady Alicia remained the head of the dragon slayers and Baskor remained Primus of the Ellorian guard. The personal relationship between Pargus and Alicia deepened. The leader of the dragon slayers and the leader of the dragons, two of the most powerful forces in the Earthlands, were now bonded.

Tension had been steadily rising between Alicia and Cardinal Gregory. Poor immigrants were now streaming into Elloria pressuring the church to assist in feeding them. Now dragons were a daily part of life. Gregory cringed at the thought of emptying his coffers to care for uneducated, needy people. The church saw dragons as evil and wanted no part of them. They were the devil's handmaidens. Gregory advocated for their slaughter and tighter controls of the immigrants.

Despite its immense power the church could not ignore popular opinion. The commerce guilds, who had originally opposed the immigrants, were now supporting them. Population increases, it turned out, were good for business. A decade before, the church had fought a fruitless, two-year war trying to convert the heathens of the Bitterlands. To pay for the wars the church had doubled the cost of sanctifying grace. In reaction, the people rose up and almost destroyed the Basilica of Martyrs. Like bread prices, the church rulers quickly learned that sanctifying grace prices are a very delicate matter. They quickly rescinded the price increases.

The papacy's lack of response to the pestis had not gone unnoticed by the congregations. Watching the pope, the cardinals and their mistresses run away to their country palaces while thousands died had engendered bitterness. Cardinal Gregory knew perception was his greatest power. Salvation, infallibility and absolution were part of that intangible power. Gregory's job had been made easier for years because Alyos had agreed to protect Elloria with the Form of Aegis. That spell assured Gregory would not have to deal with a flock stricken by poverty or starvation. The negative reaction to the church's laissez-faire attitude toward the pestis had to be dealt with. To repair the church's image, the Cardinal offered free sanctifying grace to those who fed the newly arrived poor. It relieved him of the whole matter without affecting his purse.

The port of Themos remained quiet during the months it took to resettle refugees and train the Drakina's four thousand progeny. The gnome spies had little movement to report. Their accounts detailed the pain the Huntsmen went through withdrawing from the effects of Sanitat. Many had died while initially taking the potion and then many more had died in the agony of withdrawing from it. Reports surfaced that the majority of the Huntsmen took what gold they had been given and snuck out of the port of Themos, returning to the Bitterlands of the northeast. They had no intention of undergoing the effects of the Sanitat again and mass desertion was their solution. Kalshor Dax remained a threat but his plans had been delayed and his next scheme remained concealed. His army had been whittled down to five hundred. They became his personal guard. He still held Modren captive and he intended to use that bargaining chip soon.

Then suddenly Gamny reported to the company, "The body of Drakantos has been spotted outside the eastern gold mine with both neck horns cut deeply from her neck. She lay dead, her bones being pecked clean by vulgoyles. She had failed her master."

Kalshor had apparently given up the idea that another brood of dragon babies could be produced. Waiting another year tried his patience. These two horns would give what was left of his army of Huntsmen weeks of invincibility before they would go through withdrawal. Kalshor felt certain that as long as he held Modren captive and had the Elixir of Sanitat, Elloria would not attack again.

With a revitalized army of dragon slayers and four thousand adolescent dragons, any threat to Elloria seemed minimal. Life returned to normal in Elloria and the fear receded. Even some refugees returned to their old homes to resettle in their villages. Elloria remained the preeminent power in all the Earthlands.

Pargus the grey proposed marriage to Alicia. Alicia wanted to delay the marriage until her brother Modren was freed but Pargus insisted. Alicia wouldn't compromise and both agreed that as soon as Modren was returned they would marry. A plan to rescue Pargus was initiated. The wedding day was planned. It would be a celebration to remember. The dragons were not to be invited.

Chapter Eleven

Pargus had always wanted the dragon slayers and the dragons to be united as once force. It would consolidate his power. He had secretly wanted to have ultimate control over the Ellorian Guard but after his initial suggestion was rebuked, he stopped proffering it. Alicia had originally rejected that idea but she wanted Pargus to have the freedom to command the forces as he saw fit, even as she remained the head of the army. He kept one spotted dragon close to him at all times as his shielder. It was named Maculosis. Without asking any other soldiers to follow his example, he was presaging an omen of what was to come.

One day he called Baskor, Hugh and Thane and ordered them to select a dragon and keep it as their shielder. As the highest ranking Ellorian Guardsmen their example would be a powerful notice to the rank and file. They followed his order and selected three spotted dragons. While all the dragons remained imprinted to Pargus the dragons were compliant when Pargus required them to become shielders for the three Ellorian Guardsmen. Over the next months, every member in the Guard was given a dragon to be their shielder. While there were hushed words of opposition no one would oppose Pargus. Pargus kept Baskor close to him. Baskor remained hesitant watching so much power being concentrated in one man's hands but he honored Lady Alicia and would not oppose Pargus.

Baskor was only three years older than Pargus but he was a seasoned veteran. Baskor won and deserved the respect of the troops. He was worthy to be Primus because he had earned it. While Pargus was respected for being a Formorian and the imprinter of the dragons, it was Baskor that the troops looked up to. The troops feared Pargus for with a single word he could command four thousand dragons and wield the Forms. Pargus was young and less experienced but he had political power by virtue of his impending marriage and thus held authority over the troops.

Pargus had subtly consolidated every facet of power. He began to spend more and more time with Maculosis, his spotted dragon, ruminating in the caves near the mines. Pargus was becoming preoccupied with plotting revenge for the desecration of the Circle of Irminsul. He was angry that Alicia had not sought revenge for the death of 200 slayers and the abduction of her brother. Internally his frustration grew over the lack of retaliation toward Kalshor Dax and he obsessed with the idea of seizing control of the Port of Themos and its two gold mines. Control of the Port of Themos would give him a launch-base to wield influence over the eastern Earthlands, the Bitter regions and the surrounding seaports. That, along with control of the gold mines, would be the final pieces to place every valuable asset in the Earthlands under his control.

His future wife had no interest in manifest destiny or expansion of her empire. The welfare, feeding and happiness of the population were Alicia's only focus. She had tired of wars and battles with dragons. She spent much of her time with Gamny the gnome and Baskor working on behalf of her people. Gamny and Baskor were her only confidants. She became more and more isolated.

Pargus approached Alicia one evening and set forth a proposition. He spoke to her calmly. "I wish to take the Ellorian Guard, the ten thousand dragon slayers and the dragons and, once and for all, destroy Kalshor Dax and his Huntsmen. I will free your brother, eliminate the last threat to our people and bring peace for generations."

Lady Alicia was hesitant. She wanted no more battles. Pargus added, "There is no need for you to participate. You may remain in Elloria with Gamny and Thane to protect you."

Alicia retorted, "Pargus, there has been so much death already. So many sons have died. Can we not negotiate for Modren's return?"

Pargus said, "My Lady, this adversary is evil. His intentions and heart have been blackened by hate and power. Cruelty infests his mind. Your brother will not be returned through talk or goodwill."

Their conversation vacillated back and forth. Pargus did not want to seem unwavering or dictatorial with the ruler of Elloria so he continued to emphasize the long-term benefits of a land without malefic intruders and the return of her brother. Because of the overwhelming desire to free her brother, with great reluctance, she relented and gave her blessings.

Pargus presented the plan as having originated from Lady Alicia with the objective of ridding the land of evil and rescuing Modren. It was called The Peace Plan. Within two weeks the Ellorian Guard, the army of ten thousand dragon slayers and the four thousand dragons set off for the gold mines and the Port of Themos, with Pargus and Baskor in the lead.

Chapter Twelve

With the movement of so many men and dragons word quickly reached Kalshor Dax of their approach. Kalshor had made the decision to protect himself and allow the mines to be seized. Pargus moved his men through Antor Cleft, passing through the hills that lay east of the gold mines. It was the natural passageway from Elloria to Themos. As Pargus reached the gold mines he encountered no resistance and he left several hundred troops to secure the mines. The Ellorian guard, the slayers and the dragons headed closer to Themos.

Kalshor had not wanted confrontation. He had settled into a wealthy life of quiet splendor in the Port of Themos and was happy to allow Elloria to survive if it meant he could lead this kind of opulent life. Now he would have to defend that life. He had brewed more Elixir of Sanitat for the five hundred remaining Huntsmen and he ordered them to drink the potion. He knew that an army of five hundred immortals could devastate an army of thousands.

Kalshor sent messengers to Pargus stating that if the walls of Themos were breached, Modren would be killed. Pargus did not pass this information onto anyone else, especially not Baskor. Pargus killed the messengers.

Pargus surrounded the outside of the city with the Ellorian Guard. He ordered the guard to kill anyone leaving the city gates. Then he sent four thousand dragons into the city. Their orders were to identify the Huntsmen and deal with them. The Huntsmen were fair haired, stocky and strongly muscled. They were easily spotted. The dragons flew over the city identifying their prey. With pass after pass, they swooped down and with ten razor sharp rear talons ripped into the backs of the Huntsmen and lifted them into the sky above the city. You could hear their screams of pain resonate all through the city. They may have been immortal but they were not immune to the anguish being inflicted upon them.

Pargus had ordered the dragons to rip each Huntsman in two. In mid-air one dragon held a Huntsman with talons deeply lodged in the back while another dragon tore the screaming head from its cervix. Blood rained from the skies above Themos. Pargus's advance orders to the dragons were now being fulfilled. The dragons then flew with the torn bodies in opposite directions out to sea and after two days dropped the remains into the depths. Even if the Huntsmen could regenerate they would be at the bottom of the sea and days from land and breathable air. It was certain death preceded by unimaginable torment as the five hundred Huntsmen bodies continuously attempted to repair themselves only to repeatedly drown in the depths of the sea. The roads of Themos were now paved in red. The dragons relished the new taste of human blood.

The Ellorian Guard and the dragon slayers watched in horror. They were seasoned war veterans but had never witnessed such utter brutality. This blood-letting was not part of the plan and the company had not been prepared.

Within three hours the city of Themos had fallen without a single Ellorian casualty. The Huntsmen were destroyed and Kalshor Dax was brought before Pargus, held by Hugh on one side and Baskor on the other side. They stood in one of the few spots not covered in blood.

Pargus, his head slightly lowered, walked around the three men slowly, methodically assessing how Kalshor would die. Maculosis stood close by sniffing at Kalshor Dax waited to see what his master had in store for the malefactor. Everyone expected a trial and prison. Ellorian law was clear. There was no death penalty.

Pargus spoke to Kalshor Dax, "You dishonored generations of my family when you desecrated the Circle of Irminsul. Your Huntsmen killed over two hundred dragon slayers. Themos and the four villages were infected with pestis and thousands died. You enslaved hundreds to mine your gold and you used forbidden spells that disrupted the Essence."

Pargus drew his long blade and held its tip next to Kalshor's throat. The blade gleamed in the sun. Baskor said, "No Pargus. This is not allowed."

Pargus gave the blade a small jerk and the blade inched into Kalshor's throat. Kalshor groaned in agony. Pargus pulled the blade halfway out. Wheezing, Kalshor gasped to take in enough air. Pargus began to put upward pressure on the blade as it began to cut a wider swath into Kalshor's throat. Hugh pushed Pargus back and Pargus pulled the blade from Kalshor's throat and stabbed it into Hugh's stomach. Hugh fell to the ground, disbelief and shock covering his face. Within seconds Hugh lay dead.

Pargus walked over to Baskor, who was still holding Kalshor. "Baskor, you remain under my command!" Baskor, having just seen his brother murdered, replied by roaring in rage and throwing the bloody, dead body of Kalshor Dax onto Pargus. Baskor had thrown the body with such force that Pargus now lay on the ground dazed and bloodied. Baskor wanted nothing more than to rip Pargus apart. Instead, he ordered his men to arrest Pargus and shackle him.

Immediately Pargus called Maculosis, his spotted dragon, to rescue him. Maculosis stood before Pargus disallowing any Ellorian Guardsmen to put a hand on him. Pargus mounted Maculosis and addressed the army and the guard," We have won a great victory today. We have rid our Earthlands of evil and carried out our queen's command. Hugh's death was an accident and all of you witnessed that unfortunate mishap. I forgive Baskor because he had just witnessed his brother's passing and was tormented with sadness. It is time to go home and rejoice."

Everyone stood in silence. Sides had just been drawn and no one knew where their loyalty stood, torn between their moral compass and their duty. Pargus continued, "The Ellorian Guard and the dragons will come with me to the Port of Themos. The dragon slayers will proceed to Elloria and return to home camp. Baskor was ordered to rejoin his remaining brother Thane in Elloria. This order stripped the Guard from its Primus. Pargus was now Primus and he controlled Themos and the gold mines. Three days later the thousand dragons who had flown off with the bodies of Huntsmen returned to Themos.

Hundreds of adult male residents in the Port of Themos were hired to join construction gangs and the city transformed itself into the jewel of the east. No expense was spared. The workers were well compensated with gold. The port was brought up to the highest standards, the buildings were all repaired and spires were encased with gold. The streets were cleaned of all traces of blood. Pargus made everyone refer to him as the great liberator. He was hailed as the city's benefactor. The Ellorian Guard, with Pargus as its Primus, had now become his personal paramilitary force.

Pargus wielded the Forms indiscriminately. He walked along the boulevard and chanted, "Flos Partitus," and thousands of flowers would bloom. He would walk to the harbor where fishermen were casting their nets and chant, "Piscus Multitudinos," and the nets would be filled to overflowing with fish. He once walked up to a man afflicted with leprosy in the busy street and chanted, "Sana," and the man was healed.

Everyone had expected Modren would now return to Elloria but Modren was kept in chains. Pargus had requested that Lady Alicia join him in Themos and when she refused Pargus decided that Modren was to continue his imprisonment.

The people of Themos saw Pargus as a benevolent god. This was their first encounter with an overtly powerful Formorian and they were amazed and frightened by such displays of might. They had seen his unspeakable brutality but they welcomed the destruction of Kalshor Dax and the Huntsmen. As long as the power and savagery were in their favor, as long as their wealth grew, the barbarity was justified and dismissed.

One Sunday morning edicts were posted on the Themos docks

and at all city entrances. Gnomes who were not citizens would no longer be allowed into Themos. Gnomes who were citizens would be allowed to remain but would lose the status of citizenship. Twenty percent of the population of Themos consisted of gnomes. They headed the seaman and the merchant guilds. Their ranks heavily populated the banking and trading industries. The gnomes had looked upon Kalshor Dax as a business partner. They neither opposed nor supported him. They dealt with him. Now the gnomes saw Pargus as a threat.

The heads of the seaman and merchant guilds were summoned before Lord Pargus. The two gnome leaders were informed that this was neither a discussion nor a negotiation. The crown was offering them generous compensation and their services would no longer be needed. Two humans would now head the guilds. The population was informed that the two gnomes had decided to retire in order to have more time with their families and the names of the new leaders were announced. The humans cheered the change even as the gnomes remained suspicious. The two gnomes and their families soon boarded a ship for the Bitterlands.

The main stockholder in the Port of Themos Trading Company was Ricard Callius, a gnome from a long-revered lineage and one who held great sway in the gnome community. The Callius family controlled the textile guild. His family had always been exempted from paying the pannage tolls on imported cloth. Pargus now imposed the tolls on his family. Ricard Callius knew when to protest and when to submit. This was no time to protest. Master Callius was strongly aligned with whomever held power, as his only concerns were remaining wealthy and keeping his head attached. Lord Pargus was the one person who would allow those two things to happen so Callius became his ally despite the personal abuse and the loss of citizenship.

After the slaughter of the Huntsmen, Pargus crowned himself emperor. The infamous day blood fell from the sky was renamed Independence Day. Pargus was now the sole ruler of the eastern

Earthlands and seas. Through his murder of Kalshor Dax, Pargus had seized the throne of Themos. He had also inherited the remaining Elixir of Sanitat.

Pargus had made a decision that each day he would consume one drop of the Elixir. While it was unpleasant he determined that this pace of consumption would give him immortality while negating the gruesome side effects. The Elixir effected a state of high clarity and gave him ceaseless energy that allowed him to rule with a vitality beyond human capacity. It also fueled paranoia. Now, for Pargus, fear of being overthrown and a life of self-aggrandizement dominated his days.

As a result of his addiction to Sanitat, Pargus was beginning to develop sleep terrors. He would start screaming in the middle of the night, filled with intense fear, his arms flailing, all while still asleep. He would wake up in a pool of sweat, filled with worry which prohibited him from sleeping more than a few hours each night. He developed deep, dark circles under his eyes.

Pargus sought out the necromancer Surrcon. Pargus's spies had brought Surrcon to his attention. The informants said Surrcon had the ability to communicate with the dead and predict the future. He was rumored to also possess the power to calm trepidation and dread. In a short time, Surrcon was made privy councilor. He wielded much influence over Pargus.

Surrcon was old and shriveled. He was thin and pale with only a few long strands of hair hanging from his head. He possessed malevolent black pupils surrounded by solid black iris. The furrowed brow, the pursed lips and the deeply wrinkled forehead made him look weathered. His appearance evoked dread in everyone who gazed upon him and people kept their distance. Surrcon was from Saxeus, a barren land northwest of the Glacier Mountains. Saxeuns were seen as mind manipulators.

Surrcon was always accompanied by Totem, an extremely small sailfin who was his servile minion. Sailfins are draco agamids, distant cousins of miniature dragons. They are, by far, the most intelligent of

71

their genus. They do not breathe fire. Their short transparent wings move at lightning speed, faster than a hummingbird's, and that makes them extremely adept at flying and experts at sudden, stealth maneuvers. They are always hungry and in peril of starving to death. Their clear wings are covered by hard elytron shards making it difficult to harm them, even if they are crushed or swatted.

Totem was fully grown yet could fit in Surrcon's hand. Totem was highly intelligent and could carry on conversations. Agamids are actually fairly gentile creatures who vibrate their neck fins to look menacing to an enemy. They have few defenses except their exceptional ability to fly at lightning speed. Sailfins are extremely loyal and bond with whomever feeds them. They become deeply attached to their provider. Sailfins have a most exceptional ability. They can repeat spells into the ears of unsuspecting targets.

Over the months after his appointment as privy counselor Surrcon made sure that all those who held any degree of power became indebted to him. He offered favors, bribes and pathways to promotion to everyone within the spheres of influence. His greatest grasp on power came from teaching Pargus the necro-arts.

Surrcon taught Pargus the Power of Phantasy. This was one power that subtly caused an enemy to experience the illusion of separation, confusion and forgetfulness. This power resided in its ability to alter understanding in the mind of an enemy by making them believe they were apart from all others, separate and alone. When wielded, it made an enemy's mind race with disparate and unending thoughts. In the end it made the enemy forget their purpose. Those under the spell became deranged. It was likened to creating insanity in the enemy. In reality, it was a simple spell that accelerated the pace and disorder of most people's chaotic minds.

The Power of Phantasy had both a light and a dark side. The spell Animo Tranquillium could be used to calm the mind and create silence. Surrcon covertly used this spell on Pargus so that Pargus would feel calm and empowered in Surrcon's presence. That made Pargus protective of Surrcon. The enchantment could be reversed with the spell Animo Turbatio and create a mind in chaos, a mind cut off, confounded and oblivious. These spells were not difficult to use on one individual. To use them on a mass of humans required great strength. Surrcon was training Pargus to disable an enemy through insanity.

As Pargus delved deeper and deeper into the necro-arts his ease at wielding the Forms was becoming less assured. Flowers that he materialized in the roadway meridians through wielding the Forms simply dissolved into smoke and ash one day. This was of little concern to him as his power over other men grew. One of the ways he enjoyed himself was to quietly utter the Phantasy spell, addressing it to an unsuspecting gnome and watching as the gnome lost all sense of where he was going and what he was supposed to be doing. Pargus would then ask the gnome who he was and the gnome would become unresponsive and begin to drool. To Pargus this seemed much more effective than issuing edicts. It was more efficient to simply destroy the minds of the gnomes than to send armies against them.

Pargus began to cast the spell Animo Turbatio on his Ellorian Guardsmen. He intuitively distrusted them ever since the overt opposition from Baskor, their Primus. He was subtle about it and would infest the Guard with the lightest version of the spell as they slept using his minion Totem to deliver the spell unseen. The effects were barely noticed by the Guard but the result was that over several months the Guard became agitated, conflicted and subservient. Their minds became easily influenced and Pargus was able to convince them of anything. They became malleable and, most importantly, imprintable.

Surrcon was a shadowy figure. He had arrived from the northern Earthland of Saxeus and was leader of the Council of Saxeus. This was a lost land east of the volcano Gehenna Mons. It was permeated by the vibration of the devils and Xyros dragons living in the netherworld below the volcano. Surrcon's son Meligus and several hundred Saxeun citizens had been banished underground, to the netherworld of Gehenna Mons, three years before by the Ellorians.

Their crimes were their repeated attempts to undermine the House of Elloria and seize the city's Celestine. An ill-fated coup to unseat Lady Alicia finally led to their banishment to the Sheol underworld. The remainder of the Saxeuns had been given the barren, dragon-infested, freezing northlands to resettle. The word Saxeus meant rocky and that was the perfect description of their land. The Saxeuns were left with few natural resources with which to thrive and expand. They were left with bitterness.

Everyone thought to have been involved with the coup was sentenced to the netherworld, banished to live with the devils and Xyros dragons below Gehenna Mons. Only Ailwin knew the location of the entrance to the netherworld and after the traitors were imprisoned there the entrance was sealed with the Form of impenetrability.

With few resources Surrcon turned to the dark arts and necromancy as the solution to restore his lost power and enact his revenge. He saw Pargus the grey as the susceptible pawn in his plan to avenge his bloodline's ostracism. His ultimate goal was to free his son from the Sheol of Gehenna Mons. Pargus saw Surrcon as the means to defeat the two Blue Formorians.

Surrcon was the most powerful dark wizard of the northern Earthlands. He purposely had kept an inconspicuous profile for the past few years, preparing. He had watched the events in the Earthlands play out and now saw the opportune time to emerge. Pargus planned to kill Surrcon when Ailwin and Alyos were defeated. Surrcon's plan was known only to Surrcon.

Together, Surrcon and Pargus created a mercenary army firmly under their control. The southern Earthlands had always been avoided because they were dry and barren. This land was named Haridus; thirsty. The Haridun people rapaciously sought the opportunity to emigrate north to Themos but had always been forbidden. They had been viewed as brutes who were intellectually deficient; undesirables. Now those qualities were in demand and the southern Hariduns were paid well for their brutal and supplicant nature. As Pargus had replaced Kalshor Dax as the ethnarch of Themos, the Hariduns had replaced the Huntsmen as the mercenary warriors of Themos.

Surrcon the necromancer ruled the Haridun army. The Hariduns responded well to savagery and barbarity so Pargus had allowed Surrcon great leeway in dealing with the mercenaries in whatever vicious ways he deemed appropriate to foster fear-based loyalty and discipline. When the time came Surrcon made it clear to Pargus that he wanted an unrelenting assault of brutal destruction to descend upon the dragon slayers of Elloria.

Surrcon told Pargus, "After our armies have destroyed the slayers, Elloria must be consumed by dragon fire and its ashes used to enrich the fields of our new empire. I will smite your enemies and you shall rule all the Earthlands."

This was the one-pointed purpose for which the eleven thousand Hariduns were trained. Surrcon also promised citizenship in Themos for the families of Haridun soldiers after Elloria had fallen. Of course, he had deceived them and had no intention of allowing undesirables into either Themos or Elloria.

Chapter Thirteen

The church now saw Pargus as a threat to the peace that assured the smooth inflow of tithes. Never before had they dealt with a situation where political power rested in the hands of a Formorian. The church was split on how to proceed. The Formorians were a new kind of threat. They had returned from legend and now were seizing political power. Many clergy saw the Formorians as charlatans. Others feared them, believing the songs and stories of their capabilities. Few really knew what they were dealing with. Now Pargus was reigning at the church's doorstep only miles from the papal estates. He was overtly demonstrating his influence, power and cruelty. The church could overlook Pargus's cruelty but not his power and influence.

Over the ensuing months Alicia had been summoned to the Port of Themos several more times by Pargus. Baskor the Primus and the Ellorian Guardsmen had related the stories of the rain of blood to her and how Pargus had murdered Hugh and ripped Kalshor Dax's throat open. Thane and Baskor cautioned the Lady not to go. She refused any reply to Pargus until Modren was released.

By this time a line of demarcation had firmly been drawn between Elloria and the Port of Themos. Lady Alicia and Pargus, despite a previous intention to wed, viewed each other as foes.

With the exception of the Papal lands, Pargus now wielded control over the entire eastern Earthlands, the two gold mines and the four major seaports in that region. He grew wealthy beyond any measure or rival, which was disquieting to the church. The new capital of Themos became the crowning jewel of the eastern Earthlands. Pargus avoided the land of the Huntsmen as that region now despised him and had labeled him the slaughterer of their race. It was the Huntsman who had tagged Pargus with the name the Red Emperor. The Huntsmen recast history and restored the image of Kalshor Dax as a great leader who had empowered the Huntsmen.

Pargus sent his spies into the cities and ports. He gave them his orders, "Defame the gnomes. Spread the rumor that it was the gnomes who had betrayed Elloria and allowed Kalshor Dax to steal the blue Celestine diamonds resulting in the deaths of over two hundred dragon slayers. Require the magistrates to charge and convict a gnome for every crime committed. The pubs where gnomes congregated are to be torched. Exile Ricard Callius."

For twenty generations humans and gnomes were considered equals and worked side by side. Gnomes physically resembled humans with three exceptions; they had pronounced noses, had slightly pointed ears and were generally several inches smaller than humans. Within months a word that had lain silent for almost two hundred years resurfaced; beaks. It was now the beaks who were responsible for the treachery of the diamond theft. It was the beaks who were keeping the humans from their rightful dominance in commerce. When there was a rape, a theft or a murder the humans automatically assumed it was committed by a beak and they were labeled rapists and murders. Themos, which for generations had welcomed the gnomes, was now a dangerous city for them to inhabit. Hate crimes against the gnomes skyrocketed and went unpunished. Many gnomes now immigrated to Elloria and established themselves in the commerce district or in the newfound immigration settlements outside the city gates.

While many of the central villages had been decimated and significant numbers of the population scattered, Elloria grew by leaps and bounds. Many villagers who had survived the pestis resettled in Elloria and the population, comprised of humans and gnomes, almost doubled. Despite the strain on resources and previous vociferous objections by Pargus, Alicia welcomed everyone and made sure all were taken care of. Pargus had insisted the immigrants be given only cocket, a cheap white bread that quickly turned black, but Alicia had over-ruled him and broke out finer foods from the royal store rooms. These immigrants were quickly absorbed into the fabric of the community and the city grew and continued to thrive. Now all the surrounding hills that had remained wild for centuries were converted into productive farmland and orchards. The gnomes vastly expanded trade routes and commerce boomed allowing the old and new residents to thrive.

It was during this time that Ailwin, myself and my cousin Thomas rode our steeds through the gates of Elloria. Word spread fast that Ailwin had returned and crowds formed to cheer his arrival. By the time we had reached the Celestine castle hundreds lined the street to catch a glimpse. Lady Alicia, Baskor and his brother Thane were called together and met us in the reception room of the castle. There was a great joy in this homecoming. Thomas was immediately made welcome.

Thomas was twenty now and I had just turned eighteen. Thomas was a strapping man; strong, imposing, clever and kind. He had begged to accompany us and Ailwin agreed that his resourcefulness and cunning would be important assets in what was to come. Soon after, Gamny the gnome entered and filled the room with more joy. Shortly after, Alyos the dragon whisperer arrived.

The next day an emissary from Themos arrived at the gates of Elloria. At first he was refused entry but Baskor allowed him to be escorted into chambers. The new company had been assembled for many hours, deep in discussion, when the emissary entered. The emissary did not bow and only relayed the words of Pargus. "The Lady Alicia is to return to Themos with the emissary. Each day two hundred blocks of Celestine are to be delivered to Themos and the crops from all the orchards are to be delivered to the Port of Themos when harvested." Then the emissary waited for the Lady's reply.

The great Lady rose and spoke quietly, in a measured tone. "Tell Pargus that Elloria is always willing to share its bounty with all people. He is welcome to come here and ask himself." The emissary was escorted outside the city walls and left with her reply.

Baskor spoke, "My liege, Pargus will forcibly take what he has asked for if it is not delivered."

She answered, "Yes Baskor. All indications are that Pargus will attack at some point. I have asked the high council to dissolve our engagement and prepare plans for the final protection of Elloria. Even if he were to attack and enter Elloria I want to allow him no legitimacy."

Ailwin rose, "I fear the skies are darkening with the prospect of war. Never before has Formorian fought Formorian. This will shake the Essence and threaten the very fabric of life. We must not allow this to happen."

Alyos the dragon whisperer added, "Four thousand Ussyro dragons must be reckoned with. This is my specialty and I will formulate a plan to deal with them."

Baskor chimed in, "I believe the Ellorian Guard remains loyal to Lady Alicia and will obey their Primus if they see an opening to oppose the Red Emperor. They will be my responsibility."

Lady Alicia stood and addressed the company, "I will retain command of the dragon slayers. I will work with Alyos and address the power of the Ussyro's.

Thomas and I walked over to the doorway, opened it and escorted Ricard Callius into the room. I spoke, "Master Callius wishes to offer his allegiance to this company. It is his wish to have this company accept the power and resources of the gnomes in opposition to Pargus. He has indicated that the gnomes have already formed an alliance with the Huntsmen of the Bitter Region."

Gamny stood up and with great pride said, "I will join Master Callius to protect my people and my Lady." It appeared that our company had just grown to ten. Gamny and Callius would ally Elloria with the Huntsmen, the gnomes and the four seaports.

The company agreed to meet again the next day and we all walked out into the courtyard. Suddenly the skies turned black, the winds blew. Everyone present could feel a cold darkness descend upon them. Pargus's voice resounded through the clouds. "I ask for very little to allow you to preserve your city. Do not oppose me or you will face my wrath. The Ellorian River will run red with blood if you choose to oppose me." Then the clouds evaporated and the wind subsided. Alicia was clearly shaken to hear his voice after so long. The man that she had once loved had become something unspeakable. That voice resonated with evil and any doubt of his motives was dispelled. Pargus's intentions were clear. He would not hesitate to use the Forms, the dragons, the mercenaries, the necromancer's arts, the Guardsmen and his wealth to get what he wanted. Life and death were irrelevant. His requests had morphed into threats. Threats would soon materialize into action.

Ailwin, Thomas and I formed one company to address Pargus and the Formorian threat. Ricard Callius and Gamny formed another company to forge alliances and recapture the outlying seaports. Baskor and Thane formed yet another company to re-take command of the Ellorian Guard. Alyos and the Lady Alicia formed the last company to address the threat posed by the dragons and the Huntsmen.

Alicia requested an audience with Cardinal Gregory. While always outwardly polite and supportive, they held a justifiable wariness toward each other. But now Pargus had become a common danger. For the first time since the Bitterland war, the church would commit troops and mounted dragoons to fight a mutual enemy. The church's commitment was mainly to protect its lands from an increasingly unstable invader. That worked well into Alicia's plan to trap Pargus in Antor Cleft.

Chapter Fourteen

Ricard Callius and Gamny set out for the Port of Tres, the northeast seaport controlled by Pargus. Word had been sent to the ruler of the Huntsmen asking him to rendezvous with them in Tres. It was the most distant journey of the four companies and the one that would place its members in a port controlled by their enemy.

The Huntsmen's role was to wrest control of the four seaports currently under the control of Themos and deprive Pargus of his hold on sea trade. If the four seaports could be freed and united they would present the Port of Themos with a formidable threat. Pargus would not suspect that resistance would come from the east. He would think it inefficient for Elloria to deploy resources in the eastern Earthlands so Pargus had sent no mercenaries or dragons to the eastern ports.

The Huntsmen had been waiting to exact retribution for the rain of blood and depose the Red Emperor. Callius and Gamny presented that opportunity. Callius promised the Huntsmen that when the tide had been turned and Pargus was defeated, Elloria and the Commerce Guild would welcome the Huntsmen with preferred trade status. The Huntsmen could regain access to the four seaports that had been taken by Kalshor Dax and that were now ruled by Pargus. For the Huntsmen it was a win-win chance to have their honor restored, retribution handed down to the red emperor and their economic status reinstated. They happily agreed.

Master Callius, as the former owner of the Themos Trading Company, knew the leaders of the four seaports well. They were all gnomes and had suffered under the rule of the red emperor. They had been relegated to second class non-citizens and forbidden to enter

Themos. All gnomes had been put under restricted movement status. The Huntsmen and the gnomes had a long history of cooperation and trade. Once again they held mutual objectives.

Gamny and Callius wore the ailettes of Elloria on their shoulders. They represented the arms and authority of Lady Alicia and that gave them some degree of immunity. No gnome would question them or stop them. In every bailey yard in the town of Tres, throughout the night, Gamny and Callius posted bulletins declaring that Tres and the other three seaports were now free of the red emperor's rule and were firmly in Huntsmen control. The bulletins stated that gnomes were reinstated as citizens and the taxes that had gone to Themos were suspended in perpetuity. While none of this was true nor had any of this happened, that morning brought a shift in the allegiances of the population. As the sun rose over Tres the masses were greeted with the sight of the Reeve, Pargus's representative and chief magistrate, locked in a pillory in the town square.

At midmorning a battalion of Huntsmen marched into town seizing the port. Each soldier held the Huntsman scimitar in their right hand and a halberd axe in the other. This imposing sight was met with cheers of liberation.

Three stalls were set up distributing Maslin bread made of the finest rye and wheat to all the inhabitants. The entire population rejoiced in the unexpected and unprecedented audacity of the gnomes and Huntsmen. A war of perception had been fought and won.

This plan was then repeated each day for the next three days in the other seaports. There was no time for Pargus to react and the population was uniformly behind the outcome. Not a single person was killed and the battle had been won neither through brutality nor intimidation. The four seaports were now in the hands of the new Ellorian ally and Pargus's eastern flank had been sealed off.

Chapter Fifteen

Pargus had been caught unprepared. He was determined that this would not be repeated. He wanted no part of a defensive strategy and summoned Surrcon. He would go on the offensive.

As Surrcon entered the royal chamber before him stood Pargus with Maculosis by his side. That was always an intimidating sight. Pargus was agitated, pacing rapidly. "Surrcon, I want the dragon slayers destroyed and Elloria brought to heel. Our spies report movement of the dragon slayers into Antor Cleft, led by Alicia herself. Without her Ellorian Guard these dragon slayers are her last line of defense. I will not allow us to be caught off guard again. You failed me in Tres."

Pargus uttered the words, "Morsus Gravis." Surrcon felt pain surge into every pore of his body. Even his expertise in the dark arts had not prepared him for this agony. He moaned as the excruciating suffering spread. Sweat covered his face as his torment deepened. Surrcon had no experience in wielding the Forms and this was an unexpected and frightening display of Pargus's power. For the first time Surrcon felt afraid and his hatred toward Pargus deepened and festered.

Surrcon bowed deeply in arrant supplication. For the first time in his life, he begged. "Please my liege, release me."

Pargus, with a wave of his hand, ended Surrcon's infliction. Surrcon stood straight and addressed Pargus. "We have eleven thousand Haridun mercenaries and four thousand dragons. The Lady Alicia has ten thousand dragon slayers. We should address the threat of the dragon slayers first. I will lead our armies to intercept them at Antor Cleft. Our forces easily outnumber those of Elloria.

Pargus nodded, "I do not care an iota for a Haridun life but I have grown deeply attached to my dragons. Be careful with my precious beasts." Maculosis smiled.

Surrcon bowed in recognition. He now feared Pargus as much as he hated him. The five hundred Ellorian Guard, each man flanked by his spotted dragon, led the eleven thousand mercenaries toward Antor Cleft. Thirty-five hundred additional dragons were ordered to walk behind them. While walking was not the dragon's preference Surrcon believed flying would alert the enemy. It was an impressive force. The mercenaries were expendable but they were a fierce group that had something important to gain from the extinction of their enemy. The Ellorian Guard was under the Turbatio Spell and remained compliant. The dragons were firmly imprinted to Pargus and his will. They had tasted human blood and relished more.

Chapter Sixteen

Alicia led a battalion of one thousand dragon slayers toward Antor Cleft. Baskor and Thane accompanied her. They made themselves conspicuous. They did not hide their cooking fires nor did they disguise their movements toward the Cleft. They were easily detected by Pargus's spies. The overt display of limited force wound its way into Antor Cleft. The dragon slayers were out front riding their palfrey steeds. Behind them were long horned bullocks hauling carts filled with Celestine spears, the only weapon that could penetrate dragon scales. The Themos spies reported back to Surrcon that the Lady would be taking a stand at Antor Cleft and was preparing the way for her army.

Alicia ordered her army to camp on the far western end of Antor Cleft. The location was a general's worst nightmare. It was low ground and sided on the north and south by table top ridges allowing little strategic movement. It felt as though it was a plug in the top of a bottle. Several thousand yards further in, Antor Cleft opened up to the east and south allowing freer movement and especially to the south, higher ground. Tents were erected throughout the narrow, western end. Cooking fires were started.

At night the men created embrasures in the rocky apex openings of the table top ridges. The embrasures were designed to be camouflaged openings from where the Celestine spears could be launched. Wielding the Celestine spears is what the dragon slayers were uniquely trained to do.

The Papal army of twenty-two hundred soldiers and one hundred dragoons on horseback sealed off the northeastern border that separated the Papal lands from Themos. This would pressure Pargus to turn toward Antor Cleft and fight his war there. The last thing the church wanted was damage to their property.

Meanwhile Alyos was moving the army of Ellorian dragon slayers eastward along the southern border towns of Haridus. This was a difficult passage because there were no streams and large amounts of water had to be carried for both the army and the animals. The border towns of Haridus had been emptied of men and the army of nine thousand dragon slayers encountered only women and children who offered no resistance. By creating his mercenary army Pargus had cleared the way for Alyos.

After traversing the Haridun drylands Alyos moved the troops northward toward Antor Cleft. His intention was to approach from the south after the mercenaries and dragons had entered the center of the cleft and seal them off, trapping them between Lady Alicia's western position and the eastern entry point. Just out of view of the cleft, Alyos and his troops waited for Surrcon to arrive. Alyos spent the night being updated by his spies.

One day later, Surrcon, the spellbound Ellorian guard, the eleven thousand Haridun mercenaries and the four thousand dragons entered Antor Cleft certain of their victory. In full attack mode they rushed the Ellorian western position. The Hariduns were a boisterous race and their onslaught was accompanied by loud battle cries. Their roars of confidence echoed through Antor Cleft. The anticipation of a swift victory was high. The Hariduns knew that they had four thousand dragons protecting their rear flank. They crashed into the Ellorian tents lunging with their halberds but they found the tents empty and the valley floor deserted.

The Ellorian ram horns sounded from the two flanking table top hills spooking the guardsmen's dragons. The five hundred spotted dragons that shielded each Ellorian Guardsman rose up in frightful surprise. Hundreds of Celestine spears shot from the rocky embrasures. Nearly all found their mark in a dragon's throat and the dragons began crashing down to earth flailing in pain.

Baskor moved into the mass of confused Ellorian Guardsmen

who had been freed of their dragon companions. He began issuing new commands. The guardsmen were unresponsive to the words and appeared dazed, unable to respond to orders from Baskor. The guardsmen looked for Surrcon to inspire and issue orders.

Alyos stood at the intersection of the southern and eastern hills watching the commencement of the battle as it unfolded. Facing the Ellorian Guard he uttered, "Animo Tranquillium" countering the Turbatio spell afflicting the Guardsmen. He then moved to the next line of attack. He ordered the Ellorian dragon slayers to directly engage the Haridun mercenaries. Alyos himself moved to the east to engage the dragons.

The Haridun mercenaries were, without hesitation, intent on killing the dragon slayers. The slayers were professional and disciplined. They stood their ground, armed with javelins and crossbows, holding the battlement merlon line as wave after wave of raging brutality attacked. The Hariduns were not professionally trained soldiers. They were mercenaries looking for their reward. They were familiar with one-on-one combat, not a disciplined, immovable regiment. The Hariduns were being picked off by skilled archers before they could even reach the Ellorian line. Hundreds of Hariduns fell in the initial attack. Very few Haridun axes reached their marks.

The front line was a sea of blood as bodies of Hariduns stacked one upon another. After several hours, attackers had to maneuver around countless bodies and remain vigilant not to slip in the pools of blood. The battle raged as the slayers held their position.

Alyos the dragon whisperer moved to face the dragons. The thought of killing even one dragon revolted him but these Ussyro had tasted human blood and were imprinted to a madman. There was no option but their destruction. Thousands of dragons stood ready to fly but the order did not come from Surrcon, or if it did it was not received. The Ussyro waited.

Alyos began to wield the Forms. He chanted, "Roca Pulvia." The sky turned a sanguine black and hailstones poured from the clouds pelting the dragons. The instinctual reaction from the dragons was to spread their wings and fly. But as they did the hailstones tore through their wings. The dragons were effectively grounded.

Alyos shouted, "Gelum Majstro." Ice began to form at the feet of each dragon. In terror, realizing their life-threatening predicament, the dragons began to beat their wings even as they endured the tearing of their flesh by the hailstones. The ice had frozen their hind feet to the ground. As forcefully as they tried they could not pull their hind limbs free. The freezing cold spread upward quickly quenching their inner fire. The Dragons recognized their predicament and a great agitation arose. Thousands of dragon roars filled the air. The ice began to inch higher onto their hind legs. A couple stray dragons that did escape the ice and make it into the air soon found a celestine spear lodged in their throats.

The thousands of Ussyro dragons were in a panic but could not escape their life-threatening quandary. The smell of acidic fumes was in the air as their internal fire was being extinguished by the ice. Pungent smoke began billowing from the dragon's throats. They were being asphyxiated by their own death vapor. Their eyes turned blood red as they choked on the noxious fumes. Thirty-five hundred Ussyro dragons were being suffocated by the smoke of their own quenched belly fire. The stench was unbearable. With each breath their lungs filled with the acidic smoke as their bronchi, throats and nostrils burned. They smothered on their own spent fire. Soon the dragons were silent and a pall hung over Antor Cleft.

With the effects of the Turbatio spell countered the Ellorian Guard was becoming clear headed once again and Baskor was now recognized by the guard. They welcomed their true Primus. He ordered his men to move west out of Antor Cleft.

Lady Alicia engaged with the dragon slayers and moved them from a staid battle-line position into attack mode. The mercenaries had lost nearly two thousand men. The dragon slayers had lost nearly three hundred men. Now the Haridun mercenaries were severely weakened and outflanked. They began to sense their own desperation.

They stood in pools of their countrymen's blood and were now surrounded by countless slain dragons, destroyed by their own noxious internal fumes. A disheartening despair replaced their arrogant self-assurance. They could not go west through the Ellorian guard and a thousand slayers. They could not go east and retreat back to Themos for a full division of the slayers held that position. Surrcon was nowhere to be found. They were leaderless.

Lady Alicia blew the ram's horn three times and the chaos ceased. Ellorian Guardsmen, dragon slayers and Haridun mercenaries stood silent and took heed. "No more death," she shouted. "Thousands have died today and that is more than enough for generations. Haridus needs its fathers. Elloria needs its sons. One who is not even on this battlefield today is responsible for this. He lives while you and your brothers die. Citizens of Haridus go home and turn away from death."

Upon hearing her words, the Ellorian dragon slayers opened a passage way in the middle of their ranks for the mercenaries to pass on their way south. They knew their fate would be death if they persisted, and living was their choice. They moved quickly through the opening the slayers had offered.

As the Hariduns moved south a light arose from the east that demanded attention. Above the Myros pyramid, levitating in mid-air, Pargus appeared, many times larger than normal. His appearance struck fear into all who were witnessing this. In a booming voice he addressed the victors. "You test my patience. The sorcery that protects the Myros now protects Themos. If you enter you will never exit. If you move east you die." Then his image floated to the eastern side of the pyramid and disappeared.

Chapter Seventeen

Pargus's addiction to the Sanitat, while making him physically stronger and immutable, was making him emotionally unstable. His orders seemed capricious and inconsistent. He was volatile and everyone in Themos began to fear him. Now his armies had deserted him and his dragons lay dead in the fumes of Antor Cleft. Even his Ellorian Guardsmen had returned to their true home led by their true Primus. Surrcon had disappeared. But Pargus was not deterred. He was the master of the Forms and the necro-arts. He was an emperor who no longer feared death. He still had his spies and their reports indicated Ailwin was preparing to enter Themos from the northern mountains. As word reached him of the catastrophe in Antor Cleft he did not slink away. He became enraged.

Feeling indestructible, Pargus decided to once again take the offensive. He and Maculosis would set out in the morning for the Mons Borealis, the range of low mountains north of Antor Cleft. But tonight, in a sanguine and angry mood, he made his way to the buttery where the wine was stored and numbed his racing mind. Soon he would face Ailwin but tonight he would wrap himself in richly embroidered sendal silk and be the emperor. Only Ailwin and Alyos stood in the way of his complete rule of all the Earthlands.

Mounted on his grey steed, Pargus rode north that next morning with Maculosis flying beside him. At midday he reached the Borealis River, paid the pontage fee to the bridge owner and crossed into the foothills of the Mons Borealis.

Ailwin turned toward Thomas and me and said, "Pargus is coming." Ailwin needed no spies. A blue Formorian could sense when another Formorian was nearby. For our company the additional miles to Themos would no longer have to be traversed.

Thomas moved down the road and began constructing caltrops of spiked wooden branches meant to impede Pargus's forward movement. At least the location of the encounter would be of our choosing. Never before had Formorian fought Formorian. Thomas, knowing he could not be directly in the middle of this confrontation, obscured himself in the dense thickets on the high hill above the road. He was accompanied by his longbow. It was Ailwin and myself who would face Pargus.

Pargus approached the caltrops. His horse, fearing a threat in front of him, reared up and halted. Pargus descended from his horse and turned backward, sensing the two Formorians behind him. Maculosis landed and, with absolutely no fear, turned to face us. Maculosis shot fire at Ailwin and me. Flames mixed with dragon acid burned my left arm. It was stunningly painful and I groaned in anguish, smelling my burnt flesh. Pargus smiled at Maculosis.

I uttered, "Anima Ignes." Flames rose up around both Pargus and Maculosis. It did not seem to bother the dragon but Pargus groaned and raised both hands chanting, "Peremo Stinguo." The flames retreated.

Ailwin appealed to Pargus, "Pargus, this must end. You cannot win this battle. Please stop this insanity."

In a combative tone Pargus responded, "Ailwin, you live within the restrictions imposed by past generations. I have no restrictions. I will wield all powers and will destroy anyone or anything that stands in my way."

Pargus, without hesitation, followed his threat with the chant, "Spatium Flux." The ground shook. It was as if an opaque wave of energy hit us and made the air shudder. Pargus was altering space. The Formorian code disallows Formorians to alter the essences of time, space or death but it seemed Pargus had rejected any code or boundaries and was wielding the Forms that could disrupt the essential fabric of life itself.

It felt as if the quadrant of space around us shifted and we were now inhabiting a reality just slightly off center. The problem was that it encased us and we were not able to interact outside of that space. We could see Maculosis and Pargus standing before us but we were trapped. Ailwin quickly told me, "Do not wield the Forms in here. They will affect only us."

I felt completely helpless. Spinning in my mind were the words of the Formorian sister, "The Essence will shudder, defiled by the pawn."

Only a blue Formorian can negate a disruption of the essence and reestablish balance. But from within an altered spatial continuum Ailwin couldn't do that. Thomas watched in horror as Pargus walked around the quadrant goading us to use the Forms, chiding us for siding with Elloria. Pargus told Ailwin, "You are the only thing standing in my way. I may not have the power to kill you Ailwin but I can remove you from this time. Pargus began to chant, "Temper," but before he could finish wielding the essence of time form Thomas let fly the double arrows he had placed in his crossbow. The crossbow is a powerful weapon and from this relatively close range the arrows flew with herculean force. They pierced Pargus's neck and their tips emerged out the other side. Pargus fell to the ground. Maculosis roared.

Thomas had revealed himself. Maculosis spread his wings and flew with deadly intent toward him. Thomas panicked. He ran into the trees where he thought an aerial attack could be impeded. Maculosis dove into the branches disregarding his own safety, intent on avenging his master. His wing was pierced by a branch. His flesh ripped as he struggled to reach Thomas. A dragon has no nerves along its wing shaft and this dragon was relentless, feeling no pain. Maculosis, entangled in the low trees that were protecting Thomas, repeatedly lunged at Thomas's head, jaw snapping to grasp its prey.

Blood ran profusely from the wounds in Pargus's neck as he lay on the ground. He sat up and pulled the two arrows with a great force through his neck. Blood that had been a stream became a trickle. He placed his hands over both sides of his neck adding

92

pressure to stem the flow. Rather than feeling weak from blood loss Pargus began to recover. The deep piercings began to heal themselves. He sat for several minutes recovering while the Sanitat slowly mended the devastating injury. All Ailwin and I could do was watch.

Along the lower roadway we could hear the beat of horse hoofs racing. Alyos emerged on his stallion hastening toward us. Still on his horse, Alyos chanted "Congero Effingo Herpestidae." He had manifested the Form of the geant mongoose with his utterance and a fully grown geant emerged from the ground. The geant was almost six feet long and was covered with a coarse brown-grey coat. It had flat black feet with long black claws for ripping through the toughest skin and scales. Its fearsome teeth were designed to tear out an opponent's belly quickly and efficiently. The geant, smelling dragon meat, raced toward Maculosis, attacking without need for orders.

Geant mongoose are vicious and an adult is as big as a human. They are not known to attack humans preferring dragon meat and poisonous snakes. Only geants are immune to the venom that courses through dragon blood and snake fangs.

In the trees you could hear the vicious ripping of flesh as the geant mongoose tore into the Ussyro dragon. Maculosis spewed fire and roars but the mongoose was too nimble to be targeted by the flames. The trees around them erupted into flames but the dragon was lost. Its belly had been ripped open by the geant's fangs. Thomas, shaken and delivered from certain death, emerged from his concealment and approached Alyos. He implored Alyos, "Save them."

Alyos dismounted and faced Pargus. Alyos reached out his right hand and chanted, "Non Oratio." This power made Pargus mute and he was now unable to create the vibration necessary to wield the Forms. Then Alyos chanted, "Alligatum Tellus." Pargus's hands were forced to the ground unable to remove them from the earth.

Alyos approached Ailwin and me. He touched the perimeter of the spatial rift. Alyos chanted, "Redo Substantia." He repeated it very softly over and over. The ground began to tremble as he spoke. The air around us sparked with power. We were shaken to the ground. Then suddenly the shift reversed itself and we were back in normal space.

Ailwin and I walked over to Pargus and stood glaring down upon him. Alyos, speaking to Ailwin, said "He is yours."

Ailwin responded, "We are grateful Alyos. The fabric of Essence is repaired."

It would fall to Lady Alicia to restore justice.

Chapter Eighteen

Modren was freed. The five of us, with Pargus under the control of the Forms, made our way to Elloria. After three days Pargus began his withdrawal from Sanitat. He survived only because he was a Formorian. He underwent four days of tremors, seizures, vomiting and extreme muscle pain that seemed quite unbearable. When the symptoms subsided Pargus simply stared into space. He was uncommunicative.

Our arrival in Elloria was met with a hero's welcome. A feast was held. Savory bread pudding, honey walnuts, poached pears, salmon pastries, asparagus with onion sauce and wine were served to everyone. It truly was a royal banquet. When the feast concluded I went to my quarters and collapsed in utter exhaustion. I was not feeling proud or happy. I was simply relieved. I was glad the adventure was over.

Pargus was held in solitary confinement without visitors. I was neither convinced his power had been extinguished nor was I convinced his catatonic state was real.

The Lady Alicia was now the ruler of all Earthlands and seas. She bestowed upon each member of the company a carucate, the amount of land that can be ploughed in one year. That was a significant fief conferred as a reward for service. She knew that by doing this, fallow lands would become rich and abundant and it would support the large number of tenant farmers who were without land after being displaced during the pestis. It was an immediate solution that would prove to be a boon for all concerned.

A search party was formed to track down and apprehend Surrcon the necromancer. After deserting his armies, he had returned to Saxeus to rule the governing council. Apparently he thought he would not be apprehended if he crossed the Saxeun border and would never be tried for his crimes. He was brought back to Elloria in chains, his mouth sealed to prevent him from casting spells. Totem, his sailfin agamid, was caged and brought with him. I was fascinated by the agamid and took Totem for mine. Sailfins imprint on whomever feeds them and Totem quickly acclimated to a new master.

There is no death penalty in Elloria but some demanded that Surrcon and Pargus be executed. People knew the power of the necro-arts and Surrcon was an unknown commodity, feared even in chains. Pargus was a Formorian and few people thought that either of them could be safely held in captivity. Lady Alicia would soon be required to pronounce Pargus's and Surrcon's sentences.

The next day Lady Alicia came to me for a final solution, short of execution. I appreciated her confidence in me but I always felt insufficient, too young and inexperienced to advise rulers. She was the progeny of a great family and now the sole swayer of the Earthlands. I felt intimidated. After several years I had been accepted as a Formorian. She had always noticed my hesitation with Pargus. At first that bothered her. Now she saw it as wise intuition. And Ailwin had apparently discussed my abilities to see and remember with her. She no longer wished me to take a secondary role. At nineteen years old, I was to move into the role of counselor. That seemed absurd to me but she and the company apparently saw this as destiny.

I explained to her my incredulity and distrust of Pargus's current state. I told her, "He deceived us all. He allowed himself to become attached to the dark realms of diabolism, necromancy and thaumaturgy. Those have darkened his mind. He cast aside the Formorian injunctions to protect the Essence and he weaponized it. He is responsible for the loss of thousands of lives. I know death is not allowed as a punishment but I would never trust him. I can see his power remains. Rehabilitation is not a possibility. The Sanitat has made his mind malleable and he could become easily controlled by another. There remains a most prominent danger; he can manipulate minds. Even if you isolated him under guard, he could act upon the minds of the guards and escape. So how do you keep an evil alive and neuter it?"

Lady Alicia responded, "You can cage it, drug it, cast a spell upon it."

I answered her resolutely, "I would send him to the devil. I would cast him into the Sheol, the fire caves of Gehenna Mons and seal him in. Those caves have remained reliably sealed for years. Only a blue Formorian can remove the Form of impenetrability to open them and then they could be resealed. Pargus would not have the power to open them. He would remain alive, fed by the Gehenna devils, who would welcome a new devil.

She gasped at the idea. She had once loved him and now it was being suggested he rot in the hellish realm for the rest of his life. The Gehenna Caves lie at the base of the only volcano in the earth realms on the northwest side of the Glacier Mountains. It is a land filled with tenebrosity, steeped in a blood thirsty history and filled with evil beings – a land to be avoided. And then I added, "Surrcon should be sent with him."

Lady Alicia met with the council and pronounced sentence; banishment to the Sheol of Gehenna Mons.

Because of the extreme danger that Pargus and Surrcon represented, the transfer to Gehenna Mons was ordered to proceed immediately. Totem was to accompany me. Only a blue Formorian could open the fire caves so that required Ailwin to make the journey. I would accompany him, along with a contingent of Ellorian guardsmen. Although I preferred to rest, I was happy to be with Ailwin and to see a final end to this adventure. Gamny would accompany us.

We proceeded west, staying as far south of Saxeus as possible. Gehenna Mons dominated the western skies as the terrain moved steadily upward. The landscape was filled with pines and large granite boulders. Squirrels scurried everywhere tearing pinecones apart and munching the pine nuts. Yellow butterbirds flitted through the trees adding a bright splash of color to an otherwise staid palate of brown and green. We soon reached a nameless lake and marveled at the thousands of pink flamingos wading through the shallows. Beyond this the trees were broken as if a wind had laid the land to ruin. No red deer, rabbits, pheasants, partridge or fallow deer appeared anywhere. On a decidedly positive note, no dragons appeared either, but this place was eerie and there was a palpable tension in the air.

As we rode I spoke to Ailwin. "Ailwin, I am incapable of sensing what lies ahead. It feels as if a veil has been placed over my ability to see. There is dread in the air." He simply nodded and said, "Remain vigilant."

Only Ailwin had traversed these lands before. Only he knew the location of the entrance to the caves and the spells that would open them. In order to prevent truculence, Surrcon and Pargus remained confined in a prison carriage pulled by two horses. The rest of the company all rode Ellorian white steeds. The sailfin Totem rode on my shoulder. As we approached the foothills of Gehenna Mons Ailwin appeared apprehensive. I had never seen him worried, even when we faced Pargus. He knew that imprisoning Surrcon and Pargus in the underworld was the only permanent solution, but opening the fire caves held significant risks.

After three days we reached the base of Gehenna Mons. In the morning we proceeded through an area with small volcanic cinder cone outcroppings and made our way to an area filled with caves. The smell of sulfur permeated the air. Close to mid-day Ailwin dismounted and walked over to the versant. It appeared to be a shallow depression in the rock side with no opening. He ordered Pargus and Surrcon to be taken from the prison carriage and held beside him. The sun blinded the prisoners as they emerged.

Ailwin spoke to the guards, "Throw them into the cave as soon as the opening appears. It needs to be done quickly and with precision. Once I give the order, there can be no delay. Evil lives in this mountain and nothing can be allowed to escape"

Ailwin took one step forward and began to repeatedly chant. "Antrum Templum." The hillside shook and small stones fell from the rock face. A crevice began to open accompanied by a loud clap. It widened into an open fissure. Ailwin yelled to the guards, "Now."

A black twisting smoke swirled around Surrcon and with tornado force blew the guards to the ground. Surrcon unexpectedly ran into the cave opening and a Xyros dragon appeared through the cleft opening. Its two heads reached to the ground and with its needle-like teeth picked the two guards off the ground and flung them aside. Surrcon reappeared with a Gehenna devil by his side. The devil's skin was blood red, matching his eyes. His feet were cleft hoofs and his legs were scaled. He had no hair and his teeth were rotted. Two distinct putrid smells were coming from the devil and the Xyros. This was Surrcon's territory and now the creatures of this land would serve him.

The Gehenna devil recognized Ailwin. It had been Ailwin that had imprisoned him years before. The devil knew that he could not directly kill a blue Formorian. He rushed Ailwin, leading with his elongated, razor sharp finger nails. Five nails pierced Ailwin's chest and five penetrated his neck. The real danger was not the wounds themselves but the infested purulence under the nails, a pus that would instantly infest its host. Ailwin felt the suppuration and weakened instantly.

Everything had unfolded so quickly that it felt like pandemonium. The remaining guards shot arrows at the dragon but the scales repelled them. Without Celestine tips none could penetrate.

Surrcon moved forward and grabbed the downed guardsman's sword and placed it at Ailwin's neck. Surrcon ordered me to stand back. I complied. The devil stood next to the Xyros dragon and allowed Surrcon to control the moment. Surrcon looked at the dragon and then nodded toward Pargus. Caught off-guard and not expecting an attack by his fellow conspirator, Pargus tried to morph into his Acharya grey wolf to fight the dragon, but there was not enough time. He succeeded in only shape shifting his arms and legs before the dragon ripped Pargus's head from its torso. His demise came without dignity; part wolf, part human, decapitated, covered in red blood; an end befitting the red emperor.

Without speaking I held the intention, "Aestus Calor", with my full attention on the sword. The blade and handle glowed red hot and Surrcon, his hand severely burned, was forced to drop the blade.

Staring at the devil, Ailwin spoke softly, "Lux Armiger Lapis." The satanic light bearer turned to stone as he stood before Ailwin. The devil was now granite.

Surrcon ordered the Xyros to attack. The dragon moved directly toward me, both jaws snapping, both of its heads targeting mine. His left head rammed me and I was thrown to the ground. I grabbed a handful of sand and threw it into its left eyes. I grabbed onto its right neck, wrapped my arms around it and uttered, "Exurgeo Viribus." With those words a wave of strength swept through my body. With my arms suddenly empowered I squeezed and broke the dragon's right neck. Fire spewed out of its left mouth but it was misdirected, unable to see clearly. I released the animal's neck and ran from it. Despite his weakened state, Ailwin raised his hand and spoke, "Implicitum Harenea." The ground beneath the monster liquefied, turning to quicksand. The dragon began to rapidly sink below the surface. Realizing its peril, the Xyros beat its wings. It screeched and flailed, but to no avail. Within seconds the beast was subsumed in quicksand.

Surrcon, seeing his plan unravel, ran back into the cave hoping to find back-up. Ailwin chanted, "Praecludunt." The fissure closed and the fire cave was once again sealed.

It was then I remembered the Formorian sister's words, "The deceiver will enter and the devils will call."

Gamny rushed to Ailwin's side. The infection was quickly taking its toll and Gamny was the only one with knowledge of these things. He prepared a poultice of honey, garlic, sage and ginger and pushed it into each of the ten wounds. He steeped clove and cinnamon into a tea and made Ailwin drink it. In an hour Ailwin was sweating profusely. He shook with chills. We camped at the spot so as to not tire or strain Ailwin. He slept for two days and thanks to Gamny, he recovered fully.

Chapter Nineteen

U pon our return to Elloria I had to make significant decisions. I walked in the castle gardens with Thomas, discussing the possibilities. Lady Alicia had given both Thomas and me immense tracts of farmland, but I wasn't a farmer. The idea of being a landlord to tenants did not interest me. Land was the measure of wealth and power. Neither of those were of interest to me. Having a large landholding seemed more like a burden and heavy responsibility making me feel pressured and locked into a life that didn't reflect my interests and destiny.

I gave Thomas my land and that suited him. Thomas instantly became a member of the wealthy gentry, a powerful member of the landed nobility. He built two beautifully unique, shingled, two story homes on the acreage, one with hexagon windows and one with octagon windows. He then sent for our mother Claire to live in the compound. They were now Ellorians. Thomas, following in the footsteps of Lord Leofwin of Chester Shire, became the kind overseer of one of the largest private holdings in the Earthlands.

My mother loved this arrangement. Her sons were close by. She could cook for us once again. It was her way of loving us. And she had an endless number of merchants and citizens requesting her baked goods. She became instantly famous for her culinary creations. She had always worried when her sons were gone on adventures. Now was a time for contentment and rejoicing.

Ailwin returned to the Glacier Mountains and settled back into his retirement, walking daily with his cat Filidae. He reveled in the silence and the beauty of nature. He spent many hours each day deep in union with the formless. There was no more powerful way to maintain the Balance than this. Ailwin taught that when you become the formless you touch the Essence. Then the Essence in all of life is thrilled and the formless in all beings is activated, maintaining the Balance. He wanted to return to legend and namelessness.

Lady Alicia approached me and took me aside. She spoke with great kindness. "Simon, I wish for you to become Curia Regis. I am naming you the first Magnum Consilium, chief counselor to the ruler. The time of trials is not over and there are only a few I trust to guide us through it." Knowing I could not refuse her, I reticently accepted.

For a while I stayed in Elloria, close to Thomas and my mother, which suited all three of us. I enjoyed the natural beauty of the hills, the farms and the sense of peace that I found in Elloria. Elloria had grown substantially but there was a gentle and kind sensibility there. People greeted each other. They hugged. They smiled. They offered assistance. It reminded me of Chester Shire. But I was very young and wanted something more. My curiosity made me restive with the bucolic life in the countryside.

I fed Totem five times a day and we bonded. He became my agamid and was completely loyal. I enjoyed his company and the witty remarks he would whisper into my ear. He had a bit of paranoia, a slightly bitter wit and respected no one but me, his feeder. As a result, he seldom held his tongue, quick to remark on fashion faux pas, bad taste or individual expression gone wrong. He made me laugh.

As the only Formorian in Elloria and as Curia Regis my life was consumed with helping, advising and maintaining the Balance. I would occasionally take a trip to the Glacier Mountains and visit Ailwin. He would remind me that I was a Nue'. He kept my head from getting too big. It was a time of great purpose, enjoyment and peace. But when Alyos asked me to discuss a special project with him, I leapt at the chance.

Alyos was considered the hero of Antor Cleft and the savior of Elloria. He was young, powerful, famous, respected, and a Formorian. He was given the title Mage Overlord. Next to the Lady Alicia, Alyos was politically the most powerful person in all the Earthlands and, in all practicality, the most powerful person in the land. She asked him to maintain his residency in the Port of Themos. Even though Elloria was the seat of political power, Themos was considered the seat of economic power and the crossroads for culture and trade.

Pargus had made Themos into the most beautiful city in all the Earthlands and recast the city with wide landscaped boulevards and golden domed buildings. It was simply the finest. It was ringed with stunning seascapes and the city center held vibrant restaurants, pubs, craft fairs and bakeries. There were coopers making casks, boothmen selling grains, mercers selling fine cloth, and stalls with fishmongers, fruiters and haberdashers. It was vibrant and creative and that appealed to Alyos. He gladly accepted Lady Alicia's offer to settle in to rule Themos.

Alyos made Themos the intellectual hub of the Earthlands by creating a university. Alyos wanted to restore Themos to its original Formorian glory that it possessed thousands of years ago. The Formorian Temple of Sat was restored. Most importantly he started a school for Formorians. This was the project Alyos and Ailwin invited me to join as headmaster. I accepted with relish.

The school didn't just accept applicants. It is first necessary to recognize a Formorian. Formorians are not simply educated and credentialed. They are a special breed and Alyos set out to find them. Identification can occur when a blue Formorian has a dream of recognition and they see the face of a child with blue light surrounding it. That was how Ailwin had recognized me. It also occurs when a child or adult passes the test of remembering and seeing.

Over twelve hundred applied to take the test and only four were confirmed and selected. Two others were seen in dreams of recognition by Alyos and were invited. They accepted. Those six became the first class at the Formorian Conservatory. They lived an exceptional life in residence at the Temple of Sat. Besides becoming steeped in the formless and the essence they became the holders of the power to wield the Forms. Alyos, myself and, upon special request

Ailwin, were the only instructors. As you can imagine, we all had our own distinct way of showing students how to become The Formless and wield the Forms. The Conservatory's first course was The Formorian code of Myros. The Myros Code became the essential ethical standard required of every Formorian. The Code had been engraved onto the two Pillars of Sat that graced the entrance to the temple. It centered upon maintaining the fabric of the essence and the responsibility of sustaining the Balance.

Alyos set about creating a broad roadway between Elloria and Themos, linking the cities. It ran through Antor Cleft and bordered Mirror Lake and was considered the finest causeway in all the Earthlands. It had several stone bridges to allow for easy portage without tolls. Several beautiful inns were constructed with paved inner courtyards that offered comfortable sleeping quarters. Each inn had arched porches leading to kitchens that served refined cuisine. This transportation corridor was the only one of its kind. Now the fruits, grains and vegetables of Elloria and the fish, textiles and trade of Themos were unified. This was all in addition to the wealth supplied by the two goldmines. The four villages that had been destroyed by the pestis were rebuilt and repopulated. Thus, began the golden age of the Earthlands.

Of course, Baskor married Lady Alicia. It was appropriate that the greatest military general should wed the dragon queen. He remained her protector and she remained his liege, but they laughed, they played, they swam in the Ellorian River and they, over the coming years, produced three heirs. Baskor was good for Lady Alicia. She had been traumatized by her relationship with Pargus and it was debatable if she could love, trust and confide in another man. Baskor made that all possible, and more. And he was able to have what he thought impossible. He had loved Alicia throughout his life. They had grown up together within the royal circle. They had played and talked and shared throughout their lives. But she was a royal and he was not. His father was Primus and her father was king. Lady Alicia broke tradition and married for love.

Modren became Prime Minister and handled the day-to-day affairs of state. Thane became the general of the dragon slayers. Gamny received the special title of Viceroy and became a direct representative of the queen. It was a title that held the highest respect in the Earthlands.

This was the time of Pax Elloria.

Chapter Twenty

The Temple of Sat had originally been constructed by Sat, Myros's successor. When Myros built the pyramid, it was protected with the Forms, but the temple was not protected and, over time, it fell into extreme disrepair. All that remained of the Temple were the two pillars of Sat carved with the Formorian symbols standing to the east of the pyramid. Alyos ordered the temple rebuilt from the ground up preserving the two pillars. The top symbols on the pillars represented the formless and the essence. The bottom symbols below spelled out the Myros Code.

The new temple was constructed of red granite with sixteen turrets, each capped with Celestine pyramids. The entrance road was broad enough to allow carriages to come and go at the same time. It was named Formorian Way. Near the entrance the roadway was lined with statues of the original eight Formorians, the power-wielders who were the genesis of the Formorian lineage. On the left stood life size images of Myros, Sat, Atikar and Bima. On the right stood the images of Shelia, Alina, Estrilda and Liecia. The ancient fountains that had not felt water for centuries were repaired. They graced each side of the main entrance, flanking the pillars of Sat. Silver oaks lined the entire length of Formorian Way.

Inside the Conservatory gates residents were met by an immense open courtyard. The exceptionally expansive space was needed so students could practice wielding the Forms and not cause injury or chaos to themselves, the buildings or people outside the Conservatory. Six classrooms were built along the right side of the courtyard and twenty housing units were built along the right side.

On the north side were offices, a dining hall, a kitchen, a stable, a storage room and the entrance to the Temple. There may have only been six nue's in residents but Ailwin was building toward the future.

Alyos asked me to oversee one aspect of the transformation. He said, "Simon, the Bliokasha must be transferred to the Conservatory so that the Library of the Ancients and its formulas can rest within its protected walls. The Formorian Codex of Forms and spells must be preserved and kept out of evil hands."

The Temple of Sat was not a religious temple in the standard vernacular. It was the place of power, a sanctuary. It was the main location where students and faculty practiced being The Formless. It was where the balance was sustained in equilibrium and where the fabric of the essence was preserved. Access was forbidden to everyone except the six student nue's and the Formorians. Alyos set out one primary requirement that every teacher and student attending the Conservatory spend, at minimum, one hour every day in the Temple of Sat practicing being Formless.

Together, Ailwin, Alyos and I set forth the curriculum. It consisted of the Formorian Core Courses of The Formless, The Balance, The Essence, The Myros Code and The Intention. In addition, there were courses on wielding the Forms. These consisted of wielding nature Forms, wielding earth Forms, wielding light Forms and wielding mental Forms. During the three years of training there were five specialized courses on Akasha, North Star, Inter-dimension, Continuum and Intra-dimension. It was decided that, because they were forbidden, no courses would be taught on wielding space, time and death Forms nor would courses be taught on the necro-arts. These were discussed at length in the course on the Myros Code but never practiced.

Of course, the students preferred spending their time learning how to wield the Forms. The nue's ranged in age from seven to eighteen. The four applicants were the youngest. The two dream-recognized were Julian who was twelve and Omnesta who was eighteen. They all bonded immediately because Formorians remember, so there was an immediate recognition. They saw wielding the Forms as their play. The instructors did not see it as play. This led mostly to laughter.

Omnesta was unusual in that she was neither pale, blond nor slight as were most inhabitants of the Earthlands. Her family was from a mysterious place called the Mara; many days walk south of the eastern Bitterlands. There it was warmer and sunnier. Omnesta was darker with piercing brown, earthy eyes and skin the color of the deer in the Glacier Mountains. Her hair was the color of the bark of the red oaks, a brown so dark it was near black. She was orphic and cryptic, always maintaining her place as an outlier. Her mystery always intrigued and attracted me.

It was apparent that Alyos gave special attention to the two he had dream recognized. He often walked the gardens with Julian and Omnesta after dinner. He made sure they were protected and groomed for leadership. I questioned this and one day I approached Alyos on the subject.

"Alyos, is it advisable to treat the two eldest with favoritism?"

Alyos responded, "Meet me tomorrow in the Temple of Sat, at one o'clock." He then walked away. My question remained unanswered.

I arrived early, as was my habit. I required Totem to wait outside. Alyos soon walked through the doors and into the deep silence of the temple. All the candles were lit with his words, "lucerna lumen." He did not offer pleasantries or wait for me to ask my question again. He began, "I understand your concern. Only those seen in the dream of recognition will become blue Formorians in this life. You and the two others, who were dream-recognized, have that destiny. As you saw with Pargus, there is considerable risk when so much power is held by one who does not see the blue light. While others can become Formorians and wield the Forms, only a very few have the destiny to become blue Formorians and even fewer to become Celestine Wizards. For centuries there had been no Celestine Wizards on the Earthlands until Ailwin came. He called me to help him restore the

Balance, so I came. Then you were recognized. And now we have found two more. All blue Formorians remember but only a Celestine Wizard can see everything. There is only one blue Formorian who is a Celestine Wizard; Ailwin. But now there are potentially three more blue Formorians who can become Celestine Wizards, all embodied on the Earthlands at one time."

I asked him, "Is there a purpose behind this aggregation of blue and Celestine Wizards? If it is so rare it seems there must be a design and intent behind this."

"Ailwin sees, but he does not reveal the end to others. Yes, there is a design and the balance must always be protected. The time of Pax Elloria will not always be upon the land. Creating the Formorian Conservatory held the intention of finding all the Formorians and binding that company. We will soon have a second Celestine Wizard."

The Temple suddenly glowed in the familiar blue light. Ailwin walked through the door and stood in front of me. He did not speak. This was totally unexpected to me and I was taken off guard. I felt overwhelmed by the sheer intensity of energy that was now filling the Temple and my body tingled with that power. Ailwin was no longer a body with the blue light surrounding it. He became fully the blue light, a body of blue energy. He placed his hand on the top of my head and spoke, "Sat Hum." In my mind I saw my death and knew that death no longer held power over me. In my body I saw the release of all the bonds that held my body's finest Essence together and I knew that space no longer held power over me. My eyes saw all movement stand still and I knew that time no longer held power over me. My intuition, my feelings, my mind and my body felt no separation from what was outside. What was inside and what was outside merged and I knew that 'other' no longer existed. There was only one; the formless. A small, round jewel of blue light emerged from my forehead. This blue light stood before my eyes and then it enveloped me. Secret words were spoken.

After several minutes, Ailwin removed his hand. He quietly whispered, "There are now two of us."

It wasn't until Ailwin took a step back that I recovered some semblance of normal consciousness and functionality. Alyos instructed me to remain in the Temple to assimilate the experience. Ailwin and Alyos walked outside.

I remained seated immersed in the experience of Ailwin's decent of power. As I started to stabilize in that energy bestowed upon me by Ailwin I realized that my awareness had completely shifted. I saw myself as everything. Now it was not just Alyos and Alwin who held a nimbus of blue light. Everything held an aura of blue light. I recognized that the awareness that was me was also the Essence and power of all things. Then my mind kicked in and a stark reality struck me and I walked from the temple into the courtyard where Alyos and Ailwin waited.

I bowed deeply to Ailwin in recognition of the gift he had just given me. But I couldn't hold my fear. "Surrcon has deceived us and I was the one he used to perpetrate his deception and prepare for our calamity."

Ailwin nodded. "You acted with honor. Destiny is always unfolding and you are beginning to experience the power to see from beginning to end."

I held Totem in my palm. "The truth Totem. Did you implant in my mind the suggestion that I gave to Lady Alicia to throw Pargus and Surrcon into the Sheol underworld?"

Totem winced and nodded. "Surrcon made me do it."

I was shaken at my hapless role in the deception. I explained to Ailwin and Alyos, "It was always Surrcon's goal to gain access to the Sheol netherworld and to kill Pargus. I see it clearly now. He allowed Pargus to fail at Antor Cleft and ultimately be defeated. That is why the dragons never attacked and waited, creating the opening for their destruction. Surrcon wanted Pargus dead and I set up the circumstances that allowed that. Surrcon allowed us to capture him. But most significantly he wanted access to the Sheol underworld and that could only happen if a blue Formorian was duped into opening it for him. We were all used."

Ailwin looked lovingly at me and calmly said, "My neu', you are right, but the play is not over. Now you begin to see. No one was duped. We are all characters in the play. Look ahead and you will see that there will come a time of termination of this act in the play. Everything that has happened is only allowing the proper rebalancing to occur. It may not look like that now but if you see deeply you will realize these are but waves upon the ocean of the essence moving to find Balance."

More and more images were flashing forth in my mind. I had never experienced this kind of opening before, literally watching the true past and future unfold visually in my head. It was all happening with pure clarity but I had not become accustomed to processing this yet. I was becoming overwhelmed.

Alyos put his hand on my shoulder, "Simon, allow the images to come and go. Do not fear, love or hate them. Be neutral. Simply allow. Let go of judgment and responsibility."

Ailwin spoke, "Simon, the time for your early ascension to Celestine Wizard was required to deal with what lies ahead. It is not for us to reveal to the world what is coming but we can prepare for the time of trials to prevent the Balance from becoming too unstable."

I asked Ailwin, "Why did you not allow Alyos to ascend and become a Celestine Wizard? Why me?"

Ailwin smiled and answered, "Simon, you still judge with the pairs of opposites. One is not above another. There is only one. Alyos has a different destiny and role to play. He is the hero, the paladin, the champion. He is also the creator, maintainer and destroyer. You will become the Mage Vertex, the one who will hold the Balance. You will take on my role. We are all the same but we play different parts in this play. No role is high or low. Simon, the fullness of your ascension will unfold over the next months. Allow it to happen. It can seem frightening when individuality merges into the Formless. Do not resist. Surrender to what unfolds"

We ate a small meal and I retired to my quarters. I had much to assimilate. The next morning, I felt restored. Everything had changed. My awareness and perception were drastically expanded. During waking, deep sleep and dreams I remained a watcher. I could see truth and feel inside me everything that appeared outside me. Everything I gazed upon glowed with blue light. This was going to take some time to adjust to but what was paramount now was how to deal with my new understanding and knowledge about Surrcon and how to address the threat without revealing it.

Whenever I focused my attention upon Surrcon, I could feel his Essence. It was as if I was inside of him, being him. I did not like this because it felt violating. His Essence remained pure but the energy and waves of thought that were being created within his mind were unfamiliar and unsettling. I tore my awareness from him.

Chapter Twenty-One

I sent spies to Gehenna Mons regularly. For the most part they returned with little to catch my attention. But then, in March of 1370, the spies reported that the Flamingos and butterbirds were leaving the lands surrounding the volcano. No vulgoils had been spotted. Sailfins were leaving the mountain and moving into Elloria. Ground tremors were felt as far away as Chester Shire. One earthquake caused a small avalanche on the eastern slope of the volcano. I shared these events with Alyos.

It was fortunate that both Elloria and Themos were almost four days travel to Gehenna Mons. It gave us a sense of safety. We did not feel the shaking of the earth although it was obvious that more butterbirds than usual were nesting in Elloria.

Then on April first, a day of infamy, all hell broke loose. That day is remembered as the day of fools because history remembers the Formorians as unwitting fools who were judged as unaware and unprepared.

Throughout all the eastern and western Earthlands the ground became unstable. Initially a swarm of small quakes shook various sections of the Earthlands. Then strong tremors started. In the eastern part of Elloria several buildings collapsed and fissures opened up in the roads. In Chester Shire the shaking caused barns to fall into piles of rubble. In the Glacier Mountains landslides ripped off slices of the mountain. Areas around Mirror Lake succumbed to liquefaction. Then, suddenly, a massive earthquake shook all the Earthlands. The resulting tsunami washed away parts of the Port of Tres. Then a small blast of steam and smoke erupted from the peak of Gehenna Mons.

The next day Gehenna Mons began to release her rage. A plume of sulfuric smoke, rock and ash rose seventy thousand feet into the stratosphere above Gehenna Mons. Then the tephra plume collapsed onto the eastern side of Gehenna Mons and a pyroclastic flow of steam, ash, rock and dust rushed down the mountain covering the lakes, trees and valleys with hell and yellow brimstone. Saxeus, the land closest to the volcano's eastern slopes was inundated with smoke and ash. The towns were shaken so profoundly that few buildings escaped damage. A lahar of water and mud flowed to within feet of the city's boundaries. A bulge appeared on the eastern side of Gehenna Mons.

As soon as it seemed the destruction was beginning to subside, the whole mountain shook. The eastern side of Gehenna Mons exploded in a blast that ripped the mountain apart and exposed a gigantic fissure, a chasm into the underworld. A shockwave roiled the surrounding forest searing its life. The eruption had ripped open an exit from the Sheol netherworld for the resident Hellorians. Through the smoke and ash advanced what seemed like a never-ending stream of Xyro dragons and masses of Hellorian prisoners. Their destination was Saxeus. The Hellorians, the dragons, Surrcon and the imprisoned Saxeuns were free.

Over the months that followed, the inhabitants of Saxeus and the denizens of the underworld re-established their ancestral and necromantic ties. They created a new homeland that stretched from Saxeus to Gehenna Mons. A road was built upon the mudflows that connected the newly exposed netherworld to Saxeus. They constructed a vast rock wall that lined the entire southern border with the Glacier Mountains. The eastern border was sealed off and the Rift Valley Gorge that separated Saxeus from Elloria was rimmed with patrols of Xyros dragons.

The Hellorians were energized by their new-found freedom. Excitement and enthusiasm filled their ranks. Hellorians comprised many races but were mainly the subterranean species of humans and various humans from the Earthlands that had found their way into the netherworld through banishment, imprisonment or a predilection for darkness and hellfire. Many had been imprisoned in the Sheol by Formorians. It was Surrcon who would harness this energy and create a new power in the Earthlands. Surrcon was never impatient and always held the long view. All that he had done, from his alliance with Pargus to his escape into Gehenna Mons, was calculated to restore Saxeus and free his family.

Hellorians spent months re-acclimating to the bright light and clear air. They preferred the darker and rocky locales and so were fairly comfortable settling in Saxeus. The only issues for them were their dislike of the cold and their wish to smell sulfur over flowers. As a result, there were fires burning constantly throughout Saxeus and smoke filled the air. That was quite acceptable to the new residents. The forests were being quickly felled and arable land was being created. Surrcon's pressing need was to settle and feed the underworld's former inmates. He wanted his extended family and the dragons to thrive. Everyone was willing to work as hard as necessary to turn Saxeus into a land that met all the needs of necromancers, devils, Xyro dragons, sorcerers, vulgoils, satanic priests and the commoner who felt at home with the necro-arts.

Surrcon had no pre-established conditioning of what the city should become. All he knew is that it must support his people and allow them to thrive in their own way, in their preferred conditions and under their own beliefs. The Sheol underworld and Saxeus were merged and those who preferred the depths of Gehenna Mons and those who preferred the openness of Saxeus were supported and allowed to prosper. Surrcon first and foremost was dedicated to his ancestry and his extended family. His son, Meligus, was now free.

The energy within the new Saxeun city was dynamic. For a people who had been banished, rejected, imprisoned and given no hope, this was a remarkable time to release all of their dark creativity, power, genius, imagination and ingenuity. The psychological damage deeply engrained in the minds of the inhabitants was channeled into creative work and success after success. The old were allowed the task of educating the young. The strong were allowed the task of caring for the weak. The highly intelligent were allowed the task of showing the commoner how to succeed. The bonds of community strengthened greatly. Prosperity grew rapidly and a new dark city rose from the ashes. This was Surrcon's dark brilliance.

The Ellorians watched this unfold. There were many debates concerning the rise of a dark lord and an evil people, but that was a judgment not held by everyone, especially me. Celestine Wizards do not see the world as the pairs of opposites; good and evil, happy and sad, right and wrong. For them judgment remains suspended. I was beginning to realize the Balance, the Formless and the Essence in all things. But my understanding and my transformation was far from complete.

This was very difficult for the populations of Themos and Elloria to comprehend. Many in Elloria wanted an immediate attack on the dark ones in Saxeus. The Ellorian population labeled the Saxeuns and Hellorians evil, devilish, wrong and dangerous. They were from the darkness and would infest Elloria with their wickedness and malice. The church feared the rise of Saxeus and labeled it Diabolus Terra; Devil's Land.

In Elloria, Saxeuns were maligned and labeled an enemy. The residents of Elloria remembered Surrcon's role and alliance with Pargus so there was a history that supported their judgments. For Alyos and the young Formorians, the question remained, was Surrcon's goal the destruction of Elloria and Themos or was he only concerned with ruling his people as a malevolent dictator intent on the prosperity of his subjects. Were the Saxeuns evil simply because they were different?

Chapter Twenty-Two

Thane's rise to power was significant and timely. Alicia had promoted him to lead the Dragon Slayers. The people of Elloria looked for a protector to save them from the Saxeun darkness they feared and many looked to Thane. The people related to him. He drank beer in the taverns. He used their vocabulary. He was bawdy. He vilified those who were different. Thane had risen to his level of incompetence. His ineptitude would have severe consequences.

Thane rode through the gates of Themos and directly to the Formorian Conservatory. He dismounted from his horse and knocked on the door to Alyos's private quarters. He was greeted as a welcomed friend. I had seen him entering and walked over to join them. Totem was perched on my shoulder.

Thane spoke without a verbal greeting and with a tone of warning. "Alyos, you are going to face mounting opposition if you continue along the path of non-confrontation with Saxeus."

Alyos responded, "My friend, please rest. May I get you water to drink?"

Thane was not in the mood for pleasantries, "Alyos, the people are beginning to protest in the Royal Park demanding action. The level of fear is rising and they see Surrcon as a threat to their way of life. There is talk that you are supporting Saxeus and the necro-arts."

Alyos felt some pushback was required. "Do not the people of Saxeus and Elloria both want the best for their children? Has not Saxeus sealed off their borders? They would not be doing that if they were preparing for an attack. Quite the opposite. I think it is Saxeus who fears an attack."

Thane retorted, "But Alyos, the people of Elloria are directing their anger at the Formorians now. They talk about the fact that Pargus was a Formorian. They say it is the Formorians who are preventing Elloria from mobilizing against Saxeus. They say it was the Formorians who allowed the Saxeuns to become powerful and that the Formorians were part of the plot to release Surrcon's son, Meligus. The Saxeuns are devils and necromancers and they raise their children in that religion. And Simon walks around with Surrcon's agamid on his shoulder." Totem stuck out his tongue at Thane.

Alyos responded, "Thane, it sounds like you side with the protestors? The Lady Alicia wants no more wars. She has made it clear she sides with the Formorians and is willing to talk with the Saxeuns. Do you really want another war and thousands more to die?"

Thane retorted, "Our spies have repeatedly given us trustworthy intelligence that the Saxeuns have been building up offensive positions and weapons along the Rift Valley Gorge. The people believe these reports and the promoters of war are inciting the population with these accounts. They are gaining influence. The numbers attending the protests increase each week. The church is fanning the flames of hatred against Saxeus. They want the devils destroyed. The Formorians are going from heroes to foes. Themos is further away and protected by a Celestine Wizard so you feel no immediacy. If you were in Elloria you would see it differently."

Alyos moved closer to Thane and tried to put his hand on Thane's shoulder. Thane pushed the hand away. "Don't use your Forms on me Alyos. A Formorian killed my brother. A Formorian got Elloria into the last war that cost the lives of hundreds of my friends. Now the Formorians are stopping our ruler from protecting us. I am not one of your minions. Be warned Alyos. If you come to Elloria you may no longer be considered a friend. You may find Alicia has become politically isolated and can no longer simply issue any command she wishes and expect it to be followed without question. The Slayers and the Guard are itching for battle."

119

"And what is Baskor's position in all of this?"

"Baskor is in love and will follow Alicia's orders. But others may not follow Baskor's orders."

I finally spoke up feeling into Thane's heart. "Thane, you have perverted the intelligence your spies have reported. You desire a war and have whipped up insurrection against the Formorians. You blame the Formorians for your brother's death. Your motives are clear to me."

Alyos had become visibly irritated and interjected, "You speak of betrayal, treason and revolt. You stir up the citizens into a war frenzy. You choose death over life. Be clear about your actions Thane. They have not gone unnoticed. I understand the power of fear. You are driven by fear and loss. I understand Surrcon may need to be dealt with at some point, but not by destroying the Saxeuns."

Thane seemed to change his approach. "How do we calm everyone when they fear for their survival and way of life?"

I took Totem from my shoulder and put him on the table. "Totem, you know Surrcon better than anyone. What is Surrcon planning?"

Totem snuggled uncomfortably near my arm. "Master, many people from Saxeus were imprisoned in the underworld when the Formorians first sealed the entrance to the netherworld. Surrcon's son was among them. Only a Formorian could open the entrance to the Sheol, but Surrcon knew that if he gained entry he could locate his son and wield the spells to destroy the mountain from inside, freeing Meligus and his people. His association with Pargus was planned from the start. He used me to plant the suggestion in your mind to punish him by casting him to the underworld. His entire masquerade was devised to free his heir and his fellow Saxeuns."

Thane looked at me and asked, "Do you believe this sailfin?"

"He speaks the truth," I answered. "There is always the possibility that those who were released will seek revenge. While the Saxeuns seem to exert control over the Xyros they are difficult to manage and could become a problem. I think the people of Saxeus only want to thrive. They are distinct from us in almost every way. They are dark and we are light. They prefer fire and we prefer water. They are greasy and brutal while we prefer cleanliness and are more delicate. We fear what is so different. We find the Saxeuns repulsive but they also find our appearance repulsive and weak. But I do not sense evil in their hearts."

Totem added, "Surrcon communicates with the dead, not to destroy you, but to learn and gain power from his ancestors. Surrcon needed this power because he knew that he could never convince the Formorians to open the netherworlds to free its inhabitants."

Thane spoke up, "It was the Formorians who imprisoned Surrcon's son Meligus. The father and son will seek retaliation and retribution. I suspect only Simon will have the moral authority left to change minds. We no longer trust Alyos."

Alyos became agitated. "Thane, who do you think maintains the Form of Aegis over Elloria? I regulate your perfect weather, your abundance, your rainfall. I am the one who protected you from the Ussyros, Pargus, Surrcon, the Hariduns and the Huntsmen. I destroyed your enemies at Antor Cleft. Have you forgotten? Is it you who has rewritten history in the minds of the people?"

"You spend all of your time in the Temple of Sat," Thane retorted. "You are becoming forgotten and the minds of the people are being turned against you and the other Formorians."

Alyos stood tall and raised his voice, "Do you think you could stop even one blue Formorian? Ailwin, Simon and I have secured the prosperity and safety of Elloria and Themos. We have saved all the Earthlands from destruction. We live in the Pax Elloria because of the Celestine Wizards and don't forget that."

Thane was taken back by the force of Alyos's words. They seemed like a threat and a warning – and they were. Alyos continued, becoming angrier with every word. "I should simply remove my protection and dissolve the Form of Aegus letting you deal with Saxeus in whatever way you wish. You can descend into war, death and suffering if you wish. You underestimate what war with necromancers, devils and Xyros would cost in lives and property. Without the Formorians, Elloria has no power to neutralize the necro-arts."

Thane looked at Alyos and answered, "You sound as though you think the Ellorians are the blood thirsty ones."

Like a wildfire fanned by a gust of wind Alyos's anger leapt up and consumed him. He became possessed by his rage and disgust. He pounded the table and in a loud blast of ire chanted, "Abrogo Aegis." With those two words the Form of Aegis was removed from all of Elloria. Alyos stared at Thane and spoke two more words, "leave Themos," and then he walked out of the room.

Once again I remembered the Formorian sister's prophecy, "The truth will be twisted, protection withdrawn."

I was left with Thane who sat there in shock. With a willful and recalcitrant tone Thane yelled as he walked toward the door, "You Formorians think you are the only power. You think we are dependent little worms who will beg for your help. Simon, you are a thaumaturger just like Surrcon. Keep yourself and your fellow sorcerers out of Elloria."

Totem flew to my shoulder and we followed Thane into the courtyard. Totem, who was flustered and speaking even faster than normal said, "Master, that did not go well. Surrcon is not looking for war but he is more powerful than you think. It was he who blew up Gehenna Mons. It is he who has imprinted with the thousands of Xyros dragons. It is Surrcon who has the complete loyalty of the Saxeuns and the Hellorians. The Ellorians will die with their pride."

I allowed Thane to leave on his horse and return to Elloria. I found Alyos. He was pacing in the Conservatory's main hall. I took him into an empty classroom and we talked. Alyos continued to pace. I spoke softly, "You are my friend. You are responsible for the Pax Elloria. Will you allow the Ellorians to descend into ignominy and wretchedness?" Alyos did not answer.

For now, the Earthlands prospered even as an uneasy tension separated Saxeus and Elloria. Every city reaped abundant crops, received regular rains and gentle breezes. Throughout the Earthlands people were mostly peaceful. Gehenna Mons slept once again. The seaports thrived. People flourished.

But change is inevitable and time has a way of making people forget.

Chapter Twenty-Three

Throughout the first weeks of fall a cold wind gusted unceasingly across the Ellorian landscape. That blistering gale matched the new bitterness that had infested the hearts of the Ellorians. At night the crops would freeze. The rains stopped and the grain harvest failed. The green fields and the emerald hills turned to umber. The butterbirds were supplanted by vulgoils and the deer moved higher into the mountain. Cockroaches replicated unchecked. Commerce became depressed. Immigrants were no longer welcome. Those living outside the city gates were forced to return to their old villages. The immigrants were blamed for the royal storehouses having been depleted and the current crop failure. All the anger over this was directed at Alyos for removing the Form of Aegis. The Formorians were no longer welcome in Elloria.

The Formorians had become rich and powerful. Themos was now the greatest city in the history of the Earthlands. The pyramid, the temple and the conservatory were now the center of power. The city had become the commercial, intellectual and technological hub of the Earthlands. It was the center of creativity and innovation. Superstition was being replaced by inquiry. Prosperity, health and happiness reigned over the population. It was an open society where the dialogue and practice of wisdom-arts flourished. There was a deep and growing jealousy among the Ellorians toward the residents of Themos.

After Kalshor's defeat the church was no longer receiving its tribute from Themos. Pargus had no use for a church that wielded imaginary power over a superstitious multitude. The church had seen

Pargus as a threat to its hegemony and wealth. Surrcon and the rise of necromancy had infuriated church officials. But throughout all of this the church remained silent, hoping they would not be drawn into more wars. Wars were most harmful to church wealth.

Elloria was always considered a sister-city to Themos, but when one is in pain one turns against whomever is closest. Now Ellorians were turning on Themos and the Formorians. Ellorians were also turning on Saxeus. Despite the suffering and shortages being experienced in Elloria, the ranks of the Slayers and Guardsmen were increased and military spending rose significantly. It was financed by a large loan from the Port of Tres.

Thane met with Cardinal Gregory at Gregory's residence. Thane wanted the church to side with him against the Formorians, and specifically against me. Thane bowed to the Cardinal and spoke with great respect. "My Lord, when I visited Themos it was clear that the Formorians had devised a plan to cripple Elloria. The removal of the Form of Aegis is confirmation of the Formorian betrayal. You know they have little regard for church authority. It is only the papal lands that separate Elloria and Themos. Once Elloria falls, the papal lands are next. They will use their witchcraft to usurp control over the entire western Earthlands."

Thane's approach was personal and bitter. The Cardinal cared little for this type of personal in-fighting but Gregory was intent on limiting Formorian power. As their conversation was ending, Gregory asked for what he really wanted; the state farmlands of Calfore. These were among the most valuable properties owned directly by the House of Elloria. They were not Thane's to gift, but he agreed they would be transferred to Gergory personally when Thane seized power. To secure the property, Gregory would enact the greatest punishment possible. The next day Cardinal Gregory issued the censure of excommunication, barring me from the sacraments and condemning me to an eternity in hell. The writ of excommunication was posted at the entrance to the Basilica of Martyrs in Elloria and at the entrance to the Temple of Sat in Themos:

After the judgment of the angels and with that of the saints, we excommunicate, expel, curse and damn Simon Baker, the Formorian of Themos

Baskor was caught in between his love for his brother Thane and his love for Alicia. He was hesitant to believe the Formorians were now working against Elloria. There was a growing danger for those who defended the Formorians. The power, wisdom and rule of the monarchy was beginning to be questioned openly. Alicia, feeling the political and physical threat, decided she needed to make a clandestine journey to see me. Gamny made all the arrangements and traveled with her under cover of night.

Within three days they had arrived safely and we met with loving embraces. I did not know what to expect. Just meeting with me risked her immortal soul now that I had been excommunicated. We greeted each other with great respect. She described the situation in Elloria; the discord, the growing hatred of immigrants, the distrust of outsiders, the unfounded fear toward the Saxeuns, the inter-family fighting and the rumors of a coup.

I said, "People reap what they sow. The Ellorians, led by Thane, twisted your kindness and planted the seeds of distrust. They rejected your loving protection and replaced that with suspicion. They allowed their fear to turn the Pax Elloria into deficiency, famine and need. Elloria is ready to be picked like a rotten fruit from a diseased tree."

She began to cry. I had just been bluntly honest with her, but upon seeing her tears, knew I had been insensitive and overly harsh. She responded, "Our people became spoiled and ungrateful. They forgot who and what was responsible for their prosperity. Even Baskor is supportive of Thane and I do not know if the Guardsmen and the Slayers will obey me or him. My spies say that Saxeus will attack soon but I have lost faith in their truthfulness because their allegiance to Thane is growing. They say the Saxeuns have constructed weapons of mass destruction and that the Xyros dragons are breeding at the edge of the Rift Valley, but there is no tangible proof. They say whatever furthers Thane's narrative. The more the people suffer the more they clamor for war."

I responded, "It is the cruelty of time. Once only Elloria thrived. Now only Elloria disintegrates. Saxeus, Themos, Chester Shire and the four villages prosper. The land of peace has become the land of belligerence. The lands once consumed by pestilence have become the lands of hope and prosperity. Change in Elloria is not possible without openness and trust and for now that does not exist. Sometimes people must be shocked into a new revelation and a new perspective."

She knew the truth of those words and reached out and held my arm. "Simon, only you can accomplish that now."

I spoke, "Ellorians think Saxeus is their enemy but the enemy now also includes the Formorians. We blame what is different or closest to us, so the Formorians have become the focus of their anger and we are accused of causing their suffering. I would like your permission to form a new company and take Gamny and Thomas with me to see Ailwin."

Alicia smiled. "Thank you, Simon. I will support you in any way I can."

Chapter Twenty-Four

It was time for Omnesta, the eldest and most gifted of the nues' at the Conservatory, to step up. She was much better prepared than I was at her age. She was already powerful because she had received much formal training. Alyos had given her special attention and allowed her abilities to fully express. She was potentially a blue Formorian. Despite that fact, I still considered her my novice. My attraction to her was always kept in check because of that fact. Just as Ailwin had considered me the future of the Formorians, I considered her the future. She was powerful and talented, but she was inexperienced.

Omnesta, like the others in the Conservatory, received a rare education in the seven arts; Latin, grammar, rhetoric, logic, arithmetic, geometry, astronomy and music. During this time in the Earthlands it was rare that a woman would be taught to read let alone learn the seven arts. It was even rarer that she was being groomed to lead. She was brilliant and absorbed all of her training in the arts and the Forms.

As summer was fast approaching, there would be a break in the nues' education to support the planting of the fields. I called for Omnesta and, in the presence of Alicia, we met in my quarters. I explained to her the conversation I had just had with Alicia and the situation in Elloria. She quickly recognized the urgency. I asked her to join Gamny, Thomas and myself as we journeyed to see Ailwin. She said, "Lord Simon, I am honored that you have considered me worthy to join your company."

There was a specific reason for me to select Thomas, Omnesta and Gamny for this company. Along with Alicia and Ailwin, they were the only people I completely trusted. I was learning to trust a rapidly emerging intuition. I would no longer doubt that knowing.

The next day Alicia, Gamny, Omnesta and I set out for Elloria. The beautiful roads made our journey an easy one. Alicia made sure she was not recognized. Several days later we were settled into our Ellorian homes. Omnesta stayed with my mother Claire on Thomas's farm.

On the following midmorning, Gamny, Omnesta and I met with Thomas at his home. I addressed the company. "The mission of this Ataraxis is to maintain peace. We are not commissioned to fight a war, kill a despot or take over another land. It would be easy to cast a spell or wield a Form but the goal is the elimination of the causes of war and that can only be accomplished through alliances, prosperity and a new understanding. We will go to Saxeus and befriend Surrcon and his son Meligus.

Our mission is to ally the Formorians with the Saxeuns. Now the cry for war echoes down the streets of Elloria and that call must be stifled. The alliance between Saxeus and the Formorians will end the Ellorian march to war. The Ellorians will know they would face certain defeat if they ever attacked Saxeus."

Gamny was surprised because he expected me to say that we would go to the Glacier Mountains and meet with Ailwin. He had heard me specifically tell Alicia of that intention. He inquired, "Simon, if Ellorians knew we were meeting with Surrcon they would label us traitors."

"Gamny," I said, "This is why I left Alicia with the perception that our company would be headed to the Glacier Mountains to see Ailwin. For now, this will be a clandestine mission hidden from all but this immediate company. We will be tasked with creating new alliances and a new power structure.

You must see that the surest way to eliminate an enemy is make them your friend. Surrcon was motivated by his passion to release his son Meligus and his extended family from imprisonment in Gehenna Mons. You may legitimately question his methods and how he maneuvered Pargus and the rest of us into being his unwitting accomplices, but his motives were understandable. It was Surrcon that allowed for the defeat of Pargus's army, it was Surrcon who was the clever deceiver of the Formorians and Ellorians, and it was Surrcon who was the liberator of his people. He is their hero.

The Saxeuns are very different from the people of Elloria and Themos but they are not the evil devils they are made out to be. If Ellorians label us traitors, it is not our immediate concern, but that should be avoided if possible."

Thomas, who rarely offered his opinion about political matters, asked me, "Simon, how do we restore the image of the Formorians?"

"We start by supporting the Saxeuns and offering them an alliance they cannot refuse. Except for Surrcon, the Saxeuns do not know us well. We will enter Saxeun society and mold a positive image of the Formorians. Our first priority is to end any possibility of an Ellorian invasion of Saxeus. I have made all the arrangements and you all have roles to play to convince the Saxeuns of their need to align with the Formorians."

Chapter Twenty-Five

Gamny entered Saxeus in a carriage drawn by the finest destrier horses. He was clothed in the richest silk brocade with supplementary weft of gold and silver threads woven on the royal draw looms of Tres. The Saxeuns had never seen such large horses nor such opulent fabric and they gasped at such a pretentious display of wealth. The town gossip was immediately filled with conjecture as to its cost and how one person could obtain such wealth. When they discovered Gamny was a mere servant their astonishment only grew.

Gamny presented himself as the seneschal, the head steward of the ascended Celestine Formorian, the greatest power of the Earthlands. Gamny was seeking to purchase an estate in southern Saxeus to house me during my stay in Saxeus.

There was only one estate that fit Gamny's purpose; Timberlane. It had been built over one hundred years ago as the summer home of the ruler of the northern Glacier Mountains. The estate was in a state of disrepair but the structure was magnificent, built of carved silver oak timbers, adorned with massive rock fireplaces and filled with light that entered through finely crafted leaded windows that were largely intact. The grounds had not been tended for years but they possessed great trees and lakes. Gamny purchased the estate and immediately hired over two hundred craftsmen to quickly effect a complete restoration. All workers were well fed and received double wages. Within one month the estate was ready for its residents.

Gamny met with Surrcon and Meligus. He addressed them with great courtesy. "My Lords, you are invited to greet Lord Simon and Omnesta at Timberlane tomorrow. The Couscil of Saxeus is also welcome to attend." He looked at Meligus. "Meligus, please ask Tirous to also be our guest." Tirous was Meligus's closest companion and their bond was apparent. The two men had been schoolmates in their youth. They shared childhood, insurrection and imprisonment in Gehenna Mons together. Tirous was especially tall, with strikingly defined features. He commanded a second and third look from the women present.

The following day, four royal carriages carrying only servants arrived first. Then two more carriages arrived carrying only luggage made of the finest leathers. When the baggage had been unloaded and the servants had all taken up their stations, the golden state coach, drawn by six white steeds, arrived carrying me and Omnesta.

The footman opened the carriage door and stretched out his gloved hand to assist Omnesta as she stepped out. The first shock was Omnesta's jewels; a vast array of diamonds and padparadscha sapphires. The sun made both her necklace and tiara glisten, casting rays of glimmering light everywhere. Everyone in attendance was instantly drawn to their extraordinary beauty and value. The second shock was the rich brown beauty of her skin, her eyes and her hair. Then came the amazement of her clothes. She was in spotless white; a train of pure white peacock feathers covering white silk garments. Peacocks were extremely rare and no one had seen a white peacock before. She was warmed by a white ermine cape. Tirous audibly gasped in amazement. Omnesta noticed, feeling satisfied she had achieved the desired effect.

Then I emerged. Gamny moved closer and deeply bowed as I stepped from the carriage. I was clothed in pure silver marten sable fur. Several of my fingers were adorned with large rings encrusted with diamonds. Now there was complete silence among the greeting party as they took in the overt display of wealth and power. Gamny directed me to Surrcon and Meligus, introducing the four of us. Seldom had leaders met with such obvious discrepancies. Omnesta and I were young and exuded an air of power and influence. Surrcon was old and oily. We were meticulously dressed and spotlessly clean.

Surrcon was simply attired and his face held the deep creases of a difficult past. Meligus was young and fit and was dressed more finely than his father. Surrcon was polite but it was Meligus who displayed enthusiasm and great interest. They cared little for the church's opinion of me. They saw the church as an outdated relic that wielded superstition. The church held no influence in Saxeus, especially after Cardinal Gregory had chastised Surrcon publicly and prohibited the practice of necromancy. Anyway, Saxeuns quite liked the idea of an eternity spent in the fires of hell.

Gamny led everyone through the massive carved silver oak doors to reveal the newly restored estate. Flowers adorned the spaces, filling the air with fragrance. Spotless leaded glass let in the sunlight. Buttresses and beams had all been cleaned and restored. The most beautiful linen and silk fabrics covered the furniture. It was at once tasteful, beautiful and welcoming – that is to an Ellorian. I suspect the Saxeuns felt it smelled off and was too resplendent for their taste. They preferred sulfur and stone.

I addressed Surrcon, "Thank you for your kind welcome Lord Surrcon. We are pleased to be guests in your land. Will you and your son remain for lunch?"

I was unsure how we would be perceived after Surrcon's interactions with Pargus. It had been a Formorian who had imprisoned Meligus and Tirous, along with many other Saxeuns. Surrcon responded in a soft voice, "Lord Simon, it is Saxeus who is graced by your visit. We would be honored to join you for a meal."

Lunch was a closed event attended by myself, Omnesta, Surrcon, Meligus and Tirous. As lunch was being prepared the five of us sat in the parlor and I laid out our purpose. "Lords Surrcon and Meligus, we would like to propose an alliance with your lands. The prosperity of Themos and our dynasty is the result of political cooperation and an expertise in mining. We believe we could advantage both Saxeus and Themos with this defensive alliance and a joint mining venture. You have opened Gehenna Mons and exposed the underworld but you have not discovered the ores and gems that lie in its depths. We are experts in the discovery and extrication of gold, silver, diamonds and celestine. We believe we could vastly enrich the people of Saxeus.

We also wish to offer a pledge of military cooperation to end any threat from Elloria. Peace is in both of our economic interests. We are prepared to publicly declare that any attack on Saxeus would be considered an attack upon the Formorians and Themos and we would stand with you against any attacking adversary.

We are a-political. We believe we all can thrive, but only if there is peace. We will provide both our mining expertise and our military safeguards. This alliance will create jobs for the inhabitants of Saxeus. No outside workers will be used except in areas requiring operational knowledge. We provide complete mining services; discovery, operation, management, processing and trade. We split the net profits 50-50. And we assure your country's safety."

Surrcon and Meligus had never been presented with such an opportunity nor had they imagined such a possibility. Their focus had been food, housing and the restoration of their homeland. They had been unsure of what to expect from the Formorians. Now we were offering the potential for Saxeus to economically achieve parity with Themos and assure there would be no attack from Elloria. All it would take is trust. Tirous nodded in the affirmative to Meligus. Surrcon and Meligus shook my hand and the treaty was sealed.

Within six months large deposits of gold and diamonds were being extracted, processed and sold. The first payment to Saxeus was four times the Saxeun yearly budget.

When Elloria received news of the alliance they became sullenly silent and even more fearful that the Saxeuns could destroy them. But the prospect of an attack on Saxeus vanished.

Surrcon had turned operations and responsibility of this alliance over to Meligus who showed himself to be an adept businessman and leader. Meligus was being groomed to lead. It was Meligus who had shown his people how to domesticate the aurochs, the giant bulls that roamed the wild northern earthland. That had assured a steady winter supply of meat and skins for his people. Now, with this newfound wealth, Meligus laid out plans for massive infrastructure development with new water systems, roads and farming operations. Public building and education projects were initiated. Forest restoration began. Food distribution projects assured the demise of starvation. Basic public housing was constructed to end homelessness. As the wealth poured in, the bond between Themos and Saxeus solidified with both sides benefitting beyond expectations. The fear of hunger, war and homelessness disappeared. The fear that the Ellorians would once again dominate them and imprison their families abated. Meligus kept Tirous at his side and Tirous turned out to be an expert at organization and delegation. He was the engine that quickly drove ideas into reality. Tirous had become Meligus's apprentice. Surrcon watchfully faded into the background.

At this point Meligus and his lands were benefitting so grandly through the alliance that his and his people's mistrust began to outwardly subside. Previously the Saxeuns would have revolted if they had thought that their prosperity was arising from the wizardry of a Formorian. The leaders and the people of Saxeus were now content and grateful for the swift changes that swept over their land.

Saxeuns are a reclusive people but news of what was happening within their boundaries spread to the outside Earthlands. I returned to Themos while Gamny stayed in Saxeus as the administrator, living at Timberlane. The great wealth that was accumulating was held in the coffers of the Conservatory. Tirous was put in charge of all the day to day details on behalf of the people of Saxeus.

Ellorians continued to live in their world of dwindling resources, darkening fear and suspicion. Her people were hungry, cold and problematic. Coming from a history of openness, abundance and power, it was especially demoralizing for the citizens to watch their slide into deficiency while watching Themos and Saxeus thrive.

Chapter Twenty-Six

Thane had been successful in turning the people of Elloria against the Formorians. He propagated stories that Formorians had killed his brother Hugh and hundreds of Dragon Slayers. The Formorians were also falsely accused of being the immediate cause of the suffering throughout Elloria brought about through curses and manipulation of the dark Forms. This was directly blamed on Alyos. Even I was seen as an evil wizard who was manipulating Alicia and advocating for a weak military that would allow Saxeus to attack Elloria one day. According to Thane it was I who had allowed the flood of immigrants to weaken Elloria. It was I who had convinced Alicia to empty the storehouses to feed the starving masses who were victims of the pestis. And the newest attack took the form of my direct involvement in draining the commerce and wealth from Elloria and making Themos and Saxeus the richest and most powerful Earthlands. According to Thane I had become Pargus's heir, a Formorian who was now cast as the one who had deposed Ailwin and deported him to the Glacier Mountains. Thane told the Ellorians that I was seeking alliances for the purpose of taking over Elloria.

In the face of this turmoil, Thane met with Alicia. Thane bowed and addresses her. "My lady, the church has labeled Saxeus, Diabolus Terra. They are devils and the Formorians are their allies. We must recognize this alliance and shield Elloria from their influence. Simon Baker still holds the title, Curia Regis. Our people fear his influence over you and it undermines your authority. Simon is more powerful than Pargus and is his lineage holder. The Formorians offer only destruction and devastation.

Alicia responded, "Thane, you are bold in your accusations. Temper your voice or you may find that there are greater powers than you spinning the wheel of history. Take great care Thane or it might be you who consumes the destruction."

But Thane was successfully turning the wheel of history in a false direction. It was under this cloud of suspicion and accusations that I would enter Elloria.

I had requested a meeting with Baskor, Thane and Alicia. They couldn't refuse. One of the results of Thane's false narrative was that the people feared me more than they hated me. On a positive side, the false history included countless stories of the immense power of the Formorians and so the people suspected that with a single word I could destroy them. At least, for this, I was grateful and intended to make full use of this perception.

I sent my spies into Elloria days before my arrival spreading the word that the Mage Vertex was coming. There was no mention of my name. There was a long tradition throughout the ages of the rise of the Mage Vertex and I was determined to exploit all their beliefs.

I made a grand entrance into the city. The citizens didn't want the truth. They didn't want my side of the story. They were in fear and only responded to whatever was seen as stronger than that fear. They were looking for a power that could deliver them from their misery.

As I walked down the main road leading to the city gates four Xyros dragons circled high above me swooping down to protect me from anyone who appeared to be getting too close. Totem, my agamid, was perched on my shoulder. Because he originated from Surrcon, he was especially feared. I summoned the Form of Astral Light, chanting "Astralis Coruscent." Colored, ethereal lights delicately danced in the air around me causing the residents to marvel at the heavenly luminosity. With the chant "Caerulus Laminae" I caused blue rose petals to fall from the sky in front of me so my feet would only step upon the fragrant petals. I released an angelic harmony over the city by chanting, "Canticum Angelicum." The entire city heard the beatific sound as I approached.

I walked past the Basilica of Martyrs. The acolytes were emerging from the morning's benediction and the pungent odor of frankincense emerged from the church. They witnessed my arrival and were perplexed. Was I from the heavenly hosts or was I from the devil?

As I walked by, some people cowered and some bowed in response to the sheer exhibition of power. The display was both frightening and awe-inspiring. The guards, realizing they had no power to stop me, opened the city gates and I walked toward the Celestine Palace. Upon reaching the palace doors I chanted, "Ipentur" and the palace doors shimmered. Without opening the doors, I walked through the effervescence. The Xyros dragons landed, formed a semi-circle, and in a defiant stance surrounded the palace entrance. Their eight heads were a stark reminder of who was in charge at this moment.

As I entered the royal hall I bowed to no one. I was in no mood for polite pomp or ceremony. Baskor and Thane were seated to Alicia's left. I simply began to speak, not needing recognition or permission. "Elloria is now under my care. The fields, the streams, the orchards, the mines and the air itself are under my protection. The citizens are my wards. There is no other authority except me. Beginning tomorrow you will begin to receive directions that you will follow." I had assumed the role of benevolent dictator. I chanted, "Dissipati Peribunt." Totem and I vanished.

This display had been specifically for Thane, but I must admit it upset Baskor and Alicia.

To his amazement, I appeared in Thomas' living room. He suspected my power but had little experience with wizards. We embraced, recognizing the close bond that connected us. I explained the second phase of my plan to him. He was to direct its unfolding.

The next morning one hundred and ten wagons filled with the finest grains entered the city. For the next six days this was repeated; on day two arrived the fruits, day three the vegetables, day four the fish, day five the medicines, and on day six the clothing. By the end of week one the royal storehouses were filled and distribution to those in need began.

Thomas's first directive was the opening of schools, which had been closed since the harvest failed. Each child was given meals and clothing. It was still considered unusual for children to be educated, especially girls, as all children were expected to be laborers in the fields. Children under ten were no longer allowed to be laborers. There were protests in the city over this as it meant the farmers were losing their free labor force. As soon as crowds gathered in rebellion the dragons appeared and dispersed the crowds.

Thomas' next proclamation was that all debts Elloria owed to Tres would be immediately paid in full by the Mage Vertex. The army of dragon slayers was to be placed under Baskor's command. Thane was demoted. The warmongers protested but they held no power and quickly were silenced.

Immigrants were given citizenship. Except for the crown, any privileges and prerogatives were eliminated and caste and office were now empty of power. This undermined the status quo more than any declaration but the people were enthusiastic supporters and the hierarchy that was directly affected were small in number. As they no longer controlled the armies or wealth, they submitted.

Each resident was now a citizen and each citizen received food. The basics for survival were now a right for every citizen and hunger was eliminated. People were made aware that this was only an emergency measure and in the spring the burden of prosperity would fall upon the people's intelligence and energy. Elloria would have to learn to live without the protection of the Form of Aegis but there would be Formorian support to make sure everyone had the basic necessities. Most importantly anyone wanting education or training would receive it freely. Any business that needed a supporting partner could apply for assistance in launching a new business and raising seed financing. Any existing business could apply for expansion support. Experts from the cities of Tres and Themos would be available daily to support and enact this proclamation. Only Ellorians were permitted to be business owners and all loans were directly from the crown.

The entire community was experiencing so many changes that there was a general sense of confusion as to where everyone stood. This complete sense of discombobulation was an intentional aspect of the plan. The fear of starvation evaporated.

I had met secretly with Baskor and Alicia and hammered out a treaty of protection mirroring the one which I had structured with Saxeus. Any attack on Elloria would be considered an attack on the Formorians and Themos. This alliance was soon proclaimed throughout Elloria and the citizens cheered as their fear of outside destruction abated. As calm was taking hold within Elloria I settled back into my routine at the Conservatory in Themos.

Thane knew that I would return from Themos to Elloria on the following Sunday, the Spring solstice, and he had prepared for my welcome. That Sunday, at sunrise, Ellorian guards entered Thomas's home in the early morning and arrested him. They cast him into the castle keep.

I returned that Sunday with the Xyros dragons. Thane had positioned dragon slayers in every silver oak tree that lined the city entrance. Each was armed with celestine spears and ordered to attack the dragons as soon as I had reached the road's midway point. Thomas had been taken into custody and was to be Thane's leverage. Thane preferred to avoid battle and have me surrender peacefully.

I held the image of the Xyros in my mind and chanted, "Tergora Inpenetrabiles," protecting the dragons with the Form of impenetrability. As I reached the midway point the slayers hurled their spears. As they crashed into the dragon's scales they simply bounced off and fell to earth. The slayers had never experienced this outcome before, always certain their celestine spears would penetrate their targets. They quickly descended from the trees and, fearing my retribution, ran for cover. Thane, undaunted, paraded a chained Thomas toward me. With a wave of my right hand, wielding the Form "Immunitas" the chains that held Thomas turned to grey dust and blew away in the breeze. I was still 20 feet away from Thane and

Thomas but with my left hand outstretched I directed the Form, "Habre Custodia" and raised Thane two feet into the air. He struggled and his face turned red displaying the depth of his clamber and frustration. The dragons touched down, surrounding him. They wanted to eviscerate him but I forbade it. Four dragons with eight mouths filled with nine-inch needle teeth, breathing noxious acidic fumes upon him were more than enough to subdue Thane. Baskor watched, unmoving, from the edge of the crowd. Then Baskor stepped forward and pleaded with me to release his brother. I nodded and Thane was replanted on solid ground.

A huge crowd had assembled. There was much chatter about the Mage Vertex. For the first time I directly addressed the citizens, bypassing the crown. "You desire a better life for your family and a better world for your children. Some have convinced you that threats exist from outside your borders, but the real threats are from within. Elloria is now under my protection, but not my rule. You are safe and free. You will now thrive, not because of sorcery or wizardry, but because of your enterprise and wisdom. I will return to Themos but I hold you in my awareness as a shielder and guardian. You have seen what fear, suspicion and judgment have wrought. Now see what community, cooperation and trust can create. You once lived under that mantel and you can once again." With that I vanished.

Chapter Twenty-Seven

Thane feared the citizens of Elloria would turn on him. The next morning Thane set out for Saxeus. Three days later he approached Meligus's home and requested a meeting. Meligus had never met Thane but he was aware of who he was and his opposition to the Formorians. Meligus had his own spies.

Throughout the discovery, mining, processing and marketing of the minerals, vast amounts of wealth had flowed into the Saxeun treasury and Meligus had siphoned off a substantial fortune for himself. Tirous also shared in the booty. After their incarceration in the Sheol of Gehenna Mons, Meligus trusted no one except Tirous. Meligus loved his father and viewed him as very clever but unambitious. With a guarded greeting, Meligus welcomed Thane into his home. Tirous was seated in the living room.

Thane bowed slightly and introduced himself. "I am Thane, brother of Baskor, the Primus of Elloria. I am second in command of the Ellorian Guard."

Meligus responded, "My pleasure to meet you Thane. I have been told of your encounters with Pargus, the loss of your brother Hugh and your feelings toward the Formorians. But I also know of your distrust of Saxeus and fear we will attack Elloria."

Thane had not expected Meligus to be as sharp and informed as he was. Thane's view of Saxeuns had been, for so long, negatively distorted and this was an eye-opening encounter. He had started to believe his own fabrications. "Meligus, I would like to discuss a situation with you. Are you aware that Lord Simon has done all that he has to place you in a position of submission? He has now placed this same choke collar of compliance upon Elloria. You have experienced the treachery of the Formorians first hand. You must realize that Lord Simon's intention is the complete domination of all the Earthlands."

Meligus sat there unmoving, his face reactionless. Then he answered, "Thane, has he not treated us fairly and enriched both of our peoples?" Tirous nodded.

Thane felt his personal anger and distrust arise. "Formorians appear as friends and then they show their true spots and feckless character. They use their power to take what they want through alliances, making their propositions so appealing they are impossible to turn down. Then they take over and destroy anyone who stands in their way. You and I will end our days locked in the keeps of Gehenna Mons if Lord Simon has his way."

"Thane, my father was involved with Pargus and used him. It was not Pargus who used my father. In the end, my father prevailed and Pargus was destroyed. The Saxeuns were freed from the netherworld and now thrive, surpassing the Ellorians. Pargus is dead and my father rules."

Thane replied tersely, "Meligus, your father was supremely clever. But Lord Simon is far more powerful than Pargus. He wields his power in every way; subtly through cooperation and alliances and overtly through outright control and domination. But he gets what he wants every time. Your people are now suddenly addicted to wealth and an easy life. Lord Simon has shifted the expectations of your entire society. He has made you and your people dependent upon the mines. Only Simon has the power to know where the minerals are hidden beneath Gehenna Mons. He now feeds this information to Gamny to the degree he feels your prosperity suits his plans. Simon gives you only what he wants you to have in order to increase your dependence."

"What do you want Thane? Why have you come all this way to Saxeus?"

"It is Simon's will that the Saxeuns build a land as prosperous as Themos. He also wills that Saxeuns become so dependent upon him that when the time comes Simon will rule Saxeus. He also has begun to wield control over Elloria. He comes as a rescuer and friend but I know his plan. Lord Simon obtained rule over the wealthiest earthland of all, Themos, through this kind of deception, which included the murder of my brother, the destruction of his fellow Formorian and the death of hundreds of Ellorian Guardsmen.

When his revival of Elloria and Saxeus is concluded and complete dependence is secured, Simon will enter Saxeus and Elloria and merge them with Themos, creating one earthland under his rule. But first he will make sure that they have become prosperous and dependent."

Tirous interceded, "No one but Meligus will determine the future of Saxeus. Thane, you underestimate the power of a necromancer."

Meligus realized that what Thane was saying was at least partially true. Power was still his, but he knew that his wealth was completely dependent upon the Formorians. Thane had stoked Meligus's fears and resentments that simmered just under the surface. Meligus was now feeling the Formorian deception and his own dependence. His mind was flooding with memories of those years locked in the Sheol, condemned by a Formorian. He feared his people would follow whomever assured them of maintaining their new prosperity. Meligus was already seeing how the familial bonds and civic unity were waning as wealth became the dominant priority and desire of his people. Surrcon's talk of family ties and community support were now ignored. The people universally were prioritizing their prosperity, position and power. Just as his father had used Pargus, Meligus believed he was using me to accumulate wealth and influence. Meligus's time for revenge was now at hand. The time to act was now and Thane presented that opening.

Meligus asked Thane, "What do you propose Thane?"

Thane answered, "We must sow seeds of doubt concerning Formorians among the people. We must alleviate the dependence upon Simon and create a new history for our people to believe.

Saxeus and Elloria must ally against this threat. In the end, you shall rule Saxeus and I shall rule Elloria. We must find a way to deal with the power Lord Simon possesses and eliminate the threat of the Mage Vertex.

The first step is to eliminate Gamny. Imprison him in the keeps of Gehenna Mons. Meligus, you know the breadth of the entire mining operations. You are capable of discovering ore and maintaining your land's wealth. This will begin the stripping away of the layers of dependency."

Meligus hesitated. "My father will oppose this."

Tirous spoke up, "Meligus, you are the future of Saxeus. The people look to you now. Outsiders should be expelled."

Thane responded, "Meligus, there will come a time when Saxeus will have to be independent no matter what your father's wishes. You truly are the future of Saxeus. You are the wisdom and power of your country. Now is the time to assert that authority."

Meligus took charge of the conversation. "The main question is how to deal with Lord Simon. I possess one power he does not. A necromancer holds power over the force of Axion. Simon may control the Forms which are the energy and Essence of existence but it is the Axion bonds that hold matter together. He can wield the energy and cause the Forms to operate as he sees fit, but I have the power to rip the Essence apart, to break the cement. The Axion force holds everything together and that invisible glue can be undone by releasing the bonds. Everything that Lord Simon can do, I can undo."

Meligus walked to the front door, opened it and turned toward a large red oak tree. He spoke the words, "Axino Perdere." With a full breath and strong exhale, a wind emanated from his mouth as he blew onto the tree. The tree began dissolving into light particles. Its solidity became a diffused mass, diaphanous and undefined. It took on a translucent glow and became completely transparent. Thane could see through the tree. Then it evaporated, dissolving before Thane's eyes. There was no sound, no explosion and no debris. It was simply, quietly gone.

Thane smiled. "Meligus, I can hold influence over the population and you can hold Simon in check. I will begin an influence campaign over all the residents of Saxeus and Elloria. When I am through both of our peoples will believe a new history and follow us. I will discredit the Formorians and you will show the people that they are charlatans."

"Remember Thane, with a thought I can destroy you. I cannot destroy Simon yet but I can render his power impotent. I want to rule Saxeus and Themos. I also want revenge for my imprisonment. I will see Simon and the other Formorians die slow and agonizing deaths. You will be allowed to assist me in achieving my objectives and I will assist you. You can keep Elloria but never interfere with my goals."

Thane asked, "Will you challenge Simon directly?"

Meligus responded, "Begin your preparations to change their history. I will deal with Lord Simon."

Thane shuddered at the realization of who he was dealing with. He had expected an oily, dirty and dark Saxeun with limited intelligence. What he got was a superior force. But they both wanted the same things; retaliation, revenge and power. He had to accept that Meligus would keep his word and Thane would see the Formorians destroyed. Thane believed that, in the end, he would rule Elloria.

Meligus's mind had grown restless since his liberation from Gehenna Mons. Because he had always desired his father's approval, acceptance and love, he had performed his duty in the restoration of Saxeus and tried to please his father. But the nagging memories of his years in the Sheol underworld were resurfacing with a power that tormented him. Thane had succeeded in stoking the hatred contained in those memories. It seemed like the painful memories were ripening with a new furry and his mind chewed upon their bitterness. He had money, power, influence, health and intelligence but satisfaction eluded him. His mind harassed him endlessly and he sought to placate the bedevilment of his endless thoughts. He blamed his imprisonment and his mental state on Ailwin and me.

Meligus saw me as the only thing Ailwin cherished and valued. It had been Ailwin who had imprisoned him and I would be the focus of his retribution upon Ailwin. I was like a son to Ailwin. Ailwin was old and in seclusion now and no longer felt attachment to his life on the Earthlands. His only attachment was to me. Meligus's only decision was what form should his revenge take; what would he inflict upon me.

One thing was certain; to directly confront a Blue Formorian was dangerous. If he lost a battle with me, grave consequences would ensue. Meligus understood that killing me was his most risky option. Destroying my reputation, my name and my standing would ensure I would have to experience pain, rejection and censure. Meligus wanted to see me become a pariah, an outcast in the midst of my own people. My Formorian powers would be useless when I became shunned and Ailwin would have no might or influence to alter this outcome. Ailwin would be forced to watch as the only one he valued was cast into ignominy, to watch what he loved dishonored.

Chapter Twenty-Eight

Meligus asked Thane to accompany him to the Mara, beyond the land of the Huntsmen, south of the Bitterlands. Meligus said it was there the chimera beasts lived, undisturbed by humans or gnomes. Over the next several days the two men made their way through Antor Cleft and Themos and boarded a ship for Tres. Upon their arrival in the eastern port, they hired Huntsmen scouts to guide them into the Mara hinterland.

The Mara was the mystic and inscrutable land that was Omnesta's birthplace. The Huntsmen had heard the songs of the strange people and beasts that inhabited the Mara and feared entering. They made it clear that they would lead Meligus and Thane only to the border. After that Meligus and Thane would be on their own.

The journey from Tres to the hinterland was uneventful. The land was gently sloped, crisscrossed by fresh, flowing streams. Abundant game provided sustenance. The Huntsmen were well received by all the humans they encountered and the trip to the Mara boarder was completed without incident.

At dawn the Huntsmen departed for home and Meligus and Thane were left with only a direction in which to head. As they peered toward the Eastern morning sunrise, the mountains of the Mara Bitterland were visible. They packed their gear and set out to capture their chimera. Thane had only a vague description provided by Meligus as his basis to imagine the beast. He had never seen nor heard of such a creature. He was operating on his shaky trust of Meligus. In truth, Meligus had never encountered a chimera either. When Meligus was a child his father had related the story of encountering such a monster in the Mara. Surrcon had assured Meligus the story was true and Meligus had unwavering trust in his father.

These were not particularly high mountains and the air was cold but not bitter. The earth was rocky and jagged. Little grew on the slopes. The landscape appeared as if sharp granite blades had been thrust into the sky by a hellish, underground force. Gas vents emerged from crevasses, some ignited, belching flames. Forward movement was slowed by a caution to avoid being gashed by the knifelike rocky edges. Coypu rodents scurried everywhere. They did not seem particularly fearful of human presence. There was no sign of human or gnome settlements and no sign of Omnesta's clan. This was a deserted Earthland lost in time.

Thane asked Meligus, "Meligus, where was it that you first encountered a chimera?"

Meligus answered, "I have never seen such a beast. It was my father who related the stories of their fearsomeness."

Thane became agitated. "Meligus, you take us into the unknown seeking out a deadly beast you have no certainty even exists. This chimera might be a savage brute that could kill us. You risk our lives needlessly. You waste our precious time."

Meligus responded, "Thane, you may be powerless but I am not. You may have no faith but I do. My plan will bare fruit and you will follow my orders. Now hold your tongue." Thane did not respond, but his mind chewed upon the rebuke.

The Mara lay directly before Meligus and Thane. They were now stepping on the bones of countless coypu, whitened by the sun, each engraved with gnawing teeth marks, strewn over the landscape. As the two men emerged from the jutting rock scape onto a green plane they spotted a pride of chimera; four beasts, each the size of six men. Their minds were shocked as their imagination was catching up to their reality. It was clear why the Huntsmen had refused to enter this land.

The chimera were impressive creatures but Meligus and Thane felt confused as to what they were beholding. They were not like the dragons who had elongated necks and tails. Their only resemblance to dragons was that they held fire in their bellies. The chimera were stocky and muscular with heads and bodies like lions. They had thick, short wings protruding from their sides and large, broad, clawed feet. The had goat ears and short goat fur except for the mane around their neck. The felines had snake tails. This meristem beast had a befuddling genealogy. But it was perfect for Meligus's plan.

Thane was hesitant to proceed as he had no special protective powers. Meligus, on the other hand, felt no fear and walked without hesitation toward the four chimera. The two who were standing roared as he approached, not attacking, but warning. One released a small blast of fire from its throat that was meant only to prevent a confrontation. Chimera have no natural enemies as no other animal would survive a direct confrontation. Meligus continued forward, each step measured and assured as his feet treaded over the green grass. The two chimera, now silent, faced him. The other two simply sat by unconcerned. Meligus stretched out his palm facing the creatures and spoke, "Ego Dominus." The beasts were furtive, indecisive, unreactive. Meligus repeated the command, this time loudly, with great force, and the beasts bent their two front legs bowing to their new master. Thane was awestruck at the power Meligus wielded over such animals. Meligus looked toward Thane and informed him, "They are ours now. We will take only three."

Meligus spoke again to the chimera, "Ambulo." He wanted to prevent them from flying and commanded them to walk with the men. The beasts are not good flyers as their wings are small and their girth wide. They are capable of only short flights but because of their powerful legs they could walk for indefinite periods. As the company turned toward home the fourth chimera bellowed and attacked, fumes escaping its nostrils. Meligus turned toward it, stretched out his right hand and spoke, "Axino Perdere." The beast began dissolving into light particles. It became translucent. It took on a transparent glow and dissolved.

The company of two men and three chimera took the northern

route as they returned to Tres. They traveled at night careful to avoid people and keep their captives hidden. Thane had arranged for a barge to be waiting in a private cove north of Tres. They navigated westward and returned to the Earthlands. The chimera were imprisoned in a cave protected and hidden by the spell of Occultatum.

Thane returned to Elloria and Meligus returned to Saxeus. Both were now charged with the mission of changing history; turning a fabricated story into fact. For this they each employed a cadre of twenty-one women and twenty-one men who were tasked with spreading the same story. One woman worked as a scullery maid for a prominent family in Themos. She advanced her fake causerie by telling her fellow servants that her information had come from her brother who worked at the Formorian Conservatory. "Lord Simon and Lord Alyos were enraged with the Ellorians and to punish them they removed the protection of Aegis. The two Formorian plotters are now hatching a plan to release beasts from the netherworld on All Fools Day into Themos, Elloria and Saxeus to instill dread into the inhabitants. Simon and Alyos want to set themselves up as gods to be worshipped and to be paid tribute. We will become slaves to the Formorian overlords."

This story was repeated in every pub, food stall, hostel, commercial establishment and churchyard. The news spread like wildfire. Within two days it was all the residents of the three cities were discussing. "How do we protect ourselves? How do we fight back? Should we flee? Is it better to give in without a fight? Is it possible to challenge a Formorian?" Then the gossip reached a new level. "They have always wanted to be gods. The stories of their past help and protection were all fabrications created by the Formorians to mold a benevolent fiction, in preparation for the Mage Vertex to take power." Local authorities, rulers and military generals huddled to discuss options. Even Cardinal Gregory discussed options with the Pope. You couldn't just walk in and arrest a Blue Formorian.

There was no one to gainsay this talk. The validity of it went unopposed. It was not until the third day that the erroneous facts reached Alyos and me at the Conservatory. At first Alyos smirked and thought it a joke. Then Omnesta described her experience earlier in the day as she returned from the market stalls. Residents who would seek her council in the past pelted her with stones as she walked the streets. One woman spat on her. She had no context for what was happening and kept it to herself. Now it was clear. In three days the Formorians had morphed from great beings of high wisdom who people respected and feared into enemies seeking to dominate the inhabitants. Alyos ordered the gates to the Conservatory sealed shut. All Fools Day was only seventy-two hours away.

Alyos and I were used to wielding the Forms to alter nature, conditions and circumstances but it was a Formorian rule not to alter people's minds. Never before had we seen such power to manipulate people's understanding, fealty, belief and judgment. And this was accomplished just by appealing to their internal fear and suspicion.

Alyos was furious. He was prone to rages and his tendency toward becoming infuriated had harmed the Formorian's reputation in the past. I was well aware that keeping him under control now was essential. Alyos was extremely powerful and in a rage could do irreparable damage.

After dinner, Alyos, Omnesta and I began to discuss strategy. This was a war on a completely new level and it was personally directed at us. Omnesta proffered a suggestion, "Could we mount our own campaign and show the people how you benefitted Elloria and Saxeus?"

I responded, "The people now believe these stories. They see the old history as fabrications. They will simply see our restoration of Saxeus and Elloria as more manipulation, lies and deceit. Restoring trust is a difficult thing. It is easier to tear someone down than to restore their reputation"

Alyos asked, "You keep telling me to calm down. Could we wait it out?"

I answered, "We need to discover who is behind this and what the

All Fools Day plan is." They all agreed but realized there wasn't enough time to gather the information before the festival. I planned to meet with Baskor and Alicia as soon as it was possible. Alyos and Omnesta would find Gamny and bring the company of six together.

After the discussions ended, Omnesta and I, needing to clear our heads, walked outside. No words were spoken. In the silent evening Omnesta reached for my hand and held it in hers. We walked together.

Chapter Twenty-Nine

In the dead of night on All Fools Day eve, Meligus and Thane hid one beast near the entrance to Themos. The chimera was locked in a wooden cage and concealed in obscure woodlands. At dawn the chimera was released into the streets of Themos where Meligus was stationed. The massive feline had not eaten for days. It raged with a powerful hunger. Every living thing in its path was ripped to shreds; dogs, humans, pigs, gnomes, rodents, cows and chickens. Only cats were spared. The beast plowed buildings under and indiscriminately set others ablaze. The residents had been worried what would happen on this day but their greatest hopes were dashed and their greatest fears were surpassed. They had never seen such a beast and, now that this monster had been unleashed, they fully believed the gossip that this was the sinister work of the Formorian overlords. After allowing the monster to ravage the city for four hours Meligus appeared in the town square and faced the beast. He positioned his long bow armed with a lead arrow, pulled the bowstring to its maximum limits and released the arrow. It landed deep inside the chimera's belly. This is one of the few ways to destroy a chimera as the belly fire melts the lead and destroys it from within. Hundreds witnessed this. The crowd ran to raise Meligus on their shoulders and proclaim him the city's savior.

Elloria and Saxeus were relieved that All Fools Day had passed without incident. But two days later this drama was repeated in the streets of Saxeus and two days after that, in Elloria. Word spread quickly that Meligus had repeated his heroism and now the people were safe from the revenge of the Formorians. Thane became Meligus's chief spokesman and supporter. Baskor honored his brother. Alicia kept silent.

In the middle of all of this the company of six met, helpless to intervene in events they could not stop. They felt impotent but now they knew who their enemies were. Baskor, despite outwardly supporting Thane, was tormented and conflicted. He understood Thane's desire for revenge for the killing of their brother Hugh. Alicia was a warrior and, like me, was ill prepared to deal with psychological warfare based upon deception, prevarication and lies.

Baskor sought to become a military ally with Thane but Thane had moved to Saxeus under the protection of Meligus. The people of Elloria now no longer believed that it was Surrcon who wished to destroy them but Alyos and me. Now Saxeus was their friend and Meligus their protector. The people of Elloria demanded that Alicia abdicate and Thane be made regent. She had colluded with the Formorians and was literally meeting with them while the city was attacked. The evidence was damning.

The entire western Earthlands were spun into chaos in a matter of weeks. The Formorians were no longer welcomed as the rulers of Themos. Alicia had been deposed. The Formorians were forced to abandon the Conservatory and flee Themos. All of their reputations were irreparably tarnished. They were labeled Ishmaels, outcasts. In a matter of weeks, history itself had been recast.

The news was slow to reach the depths of the Glacier Mountains where Ailwin was enjoying his retirement. While little rattled him at this point in his life, as the news sunk in he experienced the pang of heartbreak. There was no one he loved more than me. I was his nue'. He made preparations. Alicia, Alyos and I made our way to the Glacier Mountains.

Chapter Thirty

Meligus spent the next several days basking in the revelry of the Saxeun capital's celebration. Copious amounts of alcohol were consumed by the residents and they cheered him whenever he appeared in public. His father was considering stepping down as ruler in favor of his son. Surrcon was old now and was feeling a deep fatigue in his bones. He was tiring of intrigue and manipulation.

As night descended upon Saxeus, Meligus departed and began his journey to Themos. Two days later he passed through Antor Cleft, entered the borough nearest the temple complex and found discrete lodging. He kept a low profile, spoke to no one and ate alone in the shadows. His mind was spinning, filled with the images of the past few weeks. His plan had unfolded perfectly but Meligus was driven to surpass the power held by the Formorians. He didn't care to kill them. He wanted to rule them. He had seen his father manipulate the Formorians to secure his release from Gehenna Mons. He knew the Formorians were vulnerable and he intended to capitalize on their weaknesses.

Meligus had been through a great deal in his life and he seldom experienced fear, but today was an exception. He was about to put his capabilities to the most profound test of his life. That night he retired early but he found sleep illusive. He was required to take a sleeping spell to achieve slumber. The next day he would once again risk his life.

Before dawn he secreted himself to the entrance of the Myros pyramid. The entrance was guarded by two dominating stone statues of auroch bulls. There were no human guards because no one ever entered, knowing the curse that descended upon anyone foolish enough to risk crossing into that sacred space. Throughout the millennia no one who entered had ever been known to depart. At least this was the Formorian narrative. Everyone suspected that the interior was filled with the bones of those unlucky to have attempted the egress.

Meligus entered without hesitation, his heart racing. He knew he was risking his life in this attempt. The auroch bulls had always been the symbol of Saxeus and Meligus was certain the Myros pyramid was Saxeun. Meligus and all Saxeun youth were taught from birth that Myros and Sat were not Formorian or Ellorian but rather the greatest Saxeun necromancers. Just as Surrcon had freed his people from Gehenna Mons, Meligus was determined to finish freeing Themos from the Formorians and restore Saxeus to its rightful glory. It would be a Saxeun land that extended from the depths of Gehenna Mons in the west to the Port of Themos in the east. Elloria, Themos, the four villages and Chester Shire would serve Saxeus.

As Meligus entered the pyramid's vestibule he spoke, "Clara" causing the room to be softly illuminated. Meligus had never been in the interior of the Myros pyramid and what the light illuminated was totally unexpected. Painted upon the smooth stone walls were scenes of great beauty; auroch bulls roaming in green fields with butterbirds filling the skies. Silver oaks dotted the murals that depicted the rural beauty of the Earthlands. As he moved further inside an ancient artist had replicated a perfect depiction of the pyramid on the wall, exactly as the pyramid appeared from the outside. Then the vestibule opened to the royal throne room. There were no bones or rotting corpses of the treasure hunters that Meligus had expected to encounter. It was pristine, immaculate, undisturbed. The throne was an imposing mix of highly polished gold inset with diamonds that reflected the ethereal light. Great Celestine and Aura quartz crystals surrounded the perimeter of the royal chamber.

Then Meligus saw the person seated on the throne. They were unmoving and, except for the face, covered in aureate robes. In the subdued light it was difficult to make out the face clearly from a distance. Meligus walked directly in front of the person. It was a woman; ancient, yet without a wrinkle, her skin intact. Her eyes were closed. Then, under the golden robe, near her covered hand, Meligus perceived a slight movement. He took a sudden step back shocked by the thought she may be alive. Then a scarab beetle scampered out from beneath the robe's sleeve. The chafer fell to the ground and disappeared into the room's mysterious depths. Meligus assumed this woman was a grave robber who had met her fate. He reached out and with both hands snaffled the remains intending to throw them to the side of the chamber. But as he gripped her shoulders she stood up and Meligus fell to the ground in an all-consuming fear.

She walked to the darkest end of the chamber as she spoke, "I leave you to be consumed by time and join the graveyard of history."

Despite being engulfed by dread, Meligus rose and spoke, "I have not come here to rob this sacred place. I am the prince of the Saxeuns and I have entered these hallowed chambers to seek the wisdom of my sanctified ancestors."

The woman stopped and turned toward Meligus. "Your speech intrigues me. Your motives are unique and precious to me. I am Myros, the mother of the Earthlands."

Meligus asked her, "Are you a Saxeun?"

She laughed and with sternness answered, "I am Saxeun. I am Ellorian. I am Themoan, I am Haridun, I am Formorian."

Meligus understood the situation. He continued, "I wish to unite the Earthlands and spread peace to all the peoples."

"You wish to join Lord Simon's company?" she asked.

"I wish to allow everyone to join that company", Meligus answered. "I need your wisdom and power to unite all people in order to bring about the peace."

Myros spoke in a booming voice, "For centuries I have remained transcended in the Formless. And now you wish me to help you. This time is so relative and fleeting. It is the best and worst, the happiest and saddest, the strongest and weakest of times. You wish me to play in these pairs of opposites, to alter the time of trials. But this is transitory. I have seen peace and war, abundance and lack, life and death throughout the millennium. I have no interest in having a part in this play. It is you who holds an attachment to an outcome."

Meligus begged her, "Then give me the power of Myros to bring the Ataraxis, the time of peace, so the suffering of humans and gnomes may end. Give us your compassion."

"If you are truthful Meligus I will offer you a tool that in the proper hands can support the Ataraxis."

Meligus realized he had never told her his name and she knew about the Formorian plan to create the age of peace. She walked close to Meligus and reached for his right hand. She turned it palm up and gently touched the center of Meligus's palm with her index finger. Searing heat flashed through his palm and, wincing, he let out a muffled scream. The smell of his own burning flesh filled his nose, adding to his misery. He closed his eyes and felt as though he would faint. But then the pain eased and he began to feel the power of the gem Myros had burned into his hand. It was the size of a cat's eye, deep blue, perfectly round, casting a ray of cerulean light. A lazuline glow now surrounded his entire hand. The gem had not been merely inserted. It had been fused to his flesh and bone and been made part of him.

Myros explained, "Meligus, you now possess a Myros gem, a Celestine energy stone. Its energy is the foundation of all power and movement. It was this power that allowed my people to build the pyramid of Myros. It is this energy that keeps your body alive and allows the ascension of a blue Formorian into the realms of Celestine wizard. It will support your work creating the Ataraxis."

Meligus asked, "How do I use this gift. How do I access its power?"

She responded, "You will it to engage and then you surrender to it. You trust its intelligence."

"I do not understand."

She began to lead him toward the temple doors. "It is a relationship. In the end you will discover it is a relationship with yourself." And with that she ushered him out of the temple and the doors closed. Meligus turned and attempted to reopen the doors but to no avail. He hurled spells at the door without response.

Meligus had intended to go to the Conservatory and confront me and Alyos but now, because of this new experience, he decided to return to Saxeus and seek his father's council. It had been Surrcon who had exhorted him to enter the Myros pyramid. He knew his father would not have arbitrarily risked his son's life and must have been certain he would unearth a great discovery. Surrcon was certain the pyramid was Saxeun and that it held the power needed to rule all the Earthlands. Meligus always marveled at his father's clever, devious and insightful mind.

He wrapped his hand in cloth to prevent infection and hide the searing burns. Feeling a new power coursing through his arm Meligus spent the next several days riding his charger home. He kept his right hand concealed in the cuff of his garment and politely accepted the adulation of those who recognized him. He limited these engagements, focusing on his return.

By the time Meligus reached home the power of the Celestine energy stone had fully infected him. But it was not what he had expected. He did not feel ready for battle, empowered for victory, endowed to be emperor of all the Earthlands. He felt peaceful and silent, his racing mind being forced to become subdued. When he stood before his father one part of him felt remorse. The other part rebelled in a confused schizophrenic rage. He was dissociated from who he really was, fighting to restore his identity. He simply greeted his father and retreated to deal with the unfolding inner battle.

Meligus felt himself betrayed by Myros. He now believed that her solution to empowering peace was to brainwash him and coerce his power through menticide. His objective had been to empower himself and impose his rule. He labeled what she had offered him a deception and exploitation and it enraged him. He dug into his palm and ripped at the skin trying desperately to grip the gem. As his skin tore, blood began to pool in his palm and overflow onto the floor.

His anger overpowered his pain. He felt a kind of desperate claustrophobia, an overwhelming necessity to remove the force that was engulfing his mind. He felt possessed, attacked. But the gem was fused to his bone and, despite his strength and willingness to tear deeply into his own flesh, the jewel remained part of him. He was desperate and his mind began a frantic, chaotic search for more drastic alternatives. His short sword lay on the table next to him. He grabbed the arming sword, placed his hand on the table and dug the blade tip into his palm, attempting to cut the jewel loose. But it remained securely held to the bone. Uttering a guttural groan, he frantically lifted the sword high above him and, with a full brandishing swing, dismembered his right hand at the wrist. His amputated hand lay in a pool of blood on the table. Meligus let out a bloodcurdling scream as the intensity of the pain set in and the power of the gem left him. He grabbed a rope that hung from the curtain, ripped it off its anchor and tightly wound it around his arm stub stemming the spurting blood flow. He walked out of the royal quarters and into the street seeking the local doctor.

As he lay recovering in a secluded stupor, he blamed his father. It had been Surrcon who had encouraged Meligus to seek answers in the pyramid of Myros. It had been his father who had refused to build an army. And it was his father who had forbidden retribution against the Formorians despite having imprisoned his family. Meligus seethed with revenge, his mind racing with schemes of retaliation. He connived alternative strategies, discerning which would inflict the greatest pain upon the Formorians and upon Myros.

Chapter Thirty-One

I had no knowledge of Meligus's encounter with Myros. Alyos and I both held certainty that it was Meligus who had engineered the disinformation campaign against the Formorians and released the Chimera upon the three city states. Conveniently showing up in all three places to become the hero was fairly obvious to us despite the population's ready acceptance of his bravery as their savior.

I had attempted two decidedly different approaches to end the fear of the people of Saxeus and Elloria. One was to bring Saxeun prosperity through commerce and the other was to impose conditions that would alleviate Ellorian fear of starvation and defeat by supplying sufficiency. In the end both plans had ended deprivation but had failed to end fear. I felt immature and naive. I was trying unproven strategies attempting to manipulate people. So far, I had not found a solution.

Alyos was no help. He was still angry with the Ellorians and now hated Meligus for his rampant destruction of the three cities and his character assassination. At this point I probably could have convinced him to wage a holy war. Alicia appeared to have lost everything; her homeland and her throne. Even Baskor's loyalty was in question.

As we entered the Glacier Mountains the winds blew and the clouds seemed restless as they were scattered across the sky. Nature was mimicking our mood, emulating the agitated state we were all in. As we approached the familiar mountainside of my old training grounds, Ailwin stood before us with outstretched arms. The greeting was heartfelt and emotional. All three of us had been deeply affected by perfidy, defamation, treachery and loss and now we were entering the embrace of unconditional love. It made tears come to my eyes. In that moment all I wanted was to retire with Ailwin in the security, silence and beauty of these familiar lands. A deep fatigue entered me as I finally let go and allowed myself to feel safe. Ailwin allowed us a full day to recover. He felt that was quite generous.

That evening I lay on my straw bed and yearned for the life Thomas had chosen. Thomas was wedded to the land and his farm. He was living a natural, quiet life that benefitted many. I had never wanted the bucolic life of farming. It felt boring to me. But now, in my imagination, the peaceful countryside felt like a soothing and loving embrace. In my exhaustion, it felt like a deep rest. My life was driven by a force I didn't fully understand. For years now my life was one never ending battle, deception and struggle as I wandered from city to city trying to restore balance and order.

Ailwin walked over to me and smiled. He said, "You seek control. It is not unlike Meligus, but you judge your control as light and his as dark. Control is always the same, an impossible struggle of resistance against destiny. You wage war with the pairs of opposites, with peace and battle, with good and evil. Your role, your purpose, is only to maintain balance, to allow people to know the silence within themselves. When you surrender, you will realize your final ascension." Then he simply walked away and went to bed.

The next morning, breakfast awaited us when we awoke, cooked by Ailwin's own hand. After we ate, Ailwin appraised the situation. "Meligus will now consolidate power and attempt to bring Saxeus, Elloria and Themos under his control. His desire is to be emperor of all the Earthlands. Meligus has cut off his right hand and has created the narrative that it was Simon who severed his limb in a sword fight, won by Meligus. He claims he drove the Formorians into the mountains."

I asked, "How did you come by this information?"

As my words trailed off, Gamny entered the room. We were all shocked and jubilant to see his loving face. Ailwin explained, "My mission over the past week has been freeing Gamny from the keep at Gehenna Mons."

Gamny made straight for Lady Alicia and bowed deeply before her. She raised him up and embraced him. Gamny wept.

Wiping the tears from his face, Gamny spoke, "The word has spread like wildfire throughout all three city states. The people are demanding that Meligus be made emperor. He feigns modesty and pretends he will serve only at the people's behest."

"What does Meligus really want out of all of this?" Alicia asked the group.

Alyos offered his take on the situation, "Meligus has always felt inferior to his father and after his defeat by the Formorians and his incarceration in Gehenna Mons he has had something to prove. This is his revenge and payback but it's also proving his worth and superiority."

Ailwin chimed in, "Alyos is correct. There will never be enough power, enough restitution or enough retaliation for Meligus. His mind has darkened even more after he removed the Myros stone. Before, he battled within himself. His inner conflict waged the light forces of his traditions, the love of his family and state and his destiny to rule Saxeus against the unstable dark elements of victimhood, insufficiency and fear. As the dark elements began to dominate, his anger, hatred and thirst for revenge and retribution have moved to the forefront. That is who we are dealing with now. His motivations have shifted. They are personal.

He sees Myros as the symbol of the Formorians. He also blames her for the loss of his hand. He sees her as the greatest deceiver, the one power that could end his reign and the source of the Earthland's stability. Meligus sees Myros and Simon as the first and last of the lineage and, with them destroyed, the tradition of Formorian masters would end. The celestine wizards would die out because there would be no one left with the capacity to instill the descent of power that creates new Celestine Wizards. Then there would be no strength in all the Earthlands to challenge him."

So, you believe that Myros and myself are the objectives?" I asked.

Ailwin nodded in the affirmative. Ailwin explained his plan to me, Alyos, Gamny, and Alicia. The company of five would set out for Themos the morning of June seventeenth.

Chapter Thirty-Two

On June twenty first the day dawned sunny and bright. Thousands had gathered outside the Myros pyramid for the installation of Meligus as the emperor of the Earthlands. He had accomplished something no one else had been able to achieve. He had united the Earthlands. Despite the fact that this was a hurried and unexpected accession, the people were demanding his rule. They were relieved that there would be no war between Saxeus, Elloria and Themos. The commerce guilds reveled in the idea of a free trade zone that would encompass all the city states. Even Cardinal Gregory was to attend, adding his tacit approval to the coronation. In the church's view, a Saxeun was better than a Formorian. There was hope. There was no thought as to how Meligus had actually accomplished this.

The Formorians had disappeared for now and Themos would return to a city state of shipping and commerce, no longer the centerpiece of Formorian hegemony. On this day, with the Myros pyramid as the backdrop, the house of Meligus would rise. Meligus had not indicated where his new capital would be located. Most people didn't care. They simply wanted to get back to growing food and making money. As long as there was peace, as long as food was available and commerce flowed unimpeded, the people were happy. And Meligus was the one who would give them this. How he had secured power didn't matter. The people were willing to crown a devil if he could deliver their prosperity. There were a few rumors circulating about a possible deception but mores and character were unimportant to the people as long as their purses and larders were full.

A huge stage had been constructed several hundred yards from the entrance to the pyramid. People saw this display as a day engineered by Meligus to claim the ancestry linked to Myros and the ancients. That was fine with them. Meligus did not want to simply be emperor. He wanted a link to the gods and their power. He had heard the stories of Pargus and how he had crowned himself. It was a tale of self-absorbed aggrandizement that turned out poorly. He was careful not to repeat Pargus's mistakes. Meligus would allow the people to believe power flowed from them to him. He would appear as a benevolent dictator. But he would create a dynasty linked to the gods.

Thane and Tirous stood at the far-right end of the stage, inconspicuous and careful not to divert attention from Meligus. Despite the outward show of unity, citizens from the three city states hid a not too veiled rancor and animosity toward each other. Years of bad blood do not evaporate with a newfound hope. Thane had cast his loyalties with Meligus and he was careful to retain an appearance of subservience.

Baskor was in the crowd, close to Thane. The brothers remained close and the fact that Baskor had appeared to side with Thane and Meligus made the new unification possible. Meligus had indicated he was going to make Baskor the Primus of the unified Earthlands. Thane would be the regent of Elloria, subservient to the rule of the emperor. Thane and Baskor would have only titular authority. A great feast would celebrate the installation of the new ruler.

Meligus had to balance his and the people's newfound hatred for the Formorians with his desire to claim the lineage of the gods. His mental state made that difficult. Only power and revenge mattered to him now that his plan had succeeded. The stability and focus Meligus had exhibited while carrying out his plan now disintegrated inside him. Throughout the crowning, Meligus remained silent, accepting the title, crown and adulation.

As the coronation concluded nearly a hundred Xyros dragons flew overhead, frightening the crowd. The people felt the wind of their wings as they darkened the sky. Their fetid smell filled the air with noxious fumes. The twin headed monsters appeared pointed at the pyramid. Thankfully, their ears were not pulled back in attack mode. Within minutes all the Xyros had alighted on the upper reaches of the pyramid. No one had ever seen a dragon or even a vulgoil land on the pyramid. Creatures always seemed to avoid the structure. Meligus turned toward them, raised his left hand and issued his command, "Exsolvo Acidum."

Each creature, with breath after breath, blew a mist of dragon acid onto the Celestine that crowned the pyramid. The acid washed the mineral in the acrid mist and everyone watched in disbelief as the Celestine began to dissolve. The sound of hundreds of dragons snorting acidic bile onto a sacred structure was unsettling and fearful. Noxious fumes rose above the structure. Within minutes the Xyros moved down to the granite section and began to rip with their claws at the mega-stones, dislodging one at a time and causing them to tumble down the side of the structure. This spectacle went on for over an hour as citizens backed away, resigned to the fact that they would not receive their free food at the celebration. They were fearful, but unable to tear themselves away from the frenzied spectacle. The pyramid that had stood intact for centuries was being destroyed, all with the intention of forcing Myros into the open.

After significant damage had been inflicted to the monument the doors to the structure were cast open and Myros walked through the opening. She waved her right hand and the two dragons above her were thrown to the ground by the sheer power of her motion. It had been Meligus's plan to root her out of the pyramid and destroy her in front of the citizens. Meligus yelled, "Proelium Impetus" and the dragons pulled back their ears into attack mode. The dragons refocused their mission of destruction from the building to Myros. One hundred two-headed dragons dove for their prize, fighting each other for the space to inflict their damage. Myros held her hands open in front of her and a force of light surrounded her. As the Xyros attempted to seize her head with their claws, they felt blisters instantly form on their feet as their talons touched her shield of energy. Those snapping with open jaws at her face felt the pain of their lips being burnt off as their mouths reached her light.

Meligus rushed into the melee. This was a battle royal for supremacy and he was determined to achieve his goal. Meligus cast the highest spell of necromancy, "Proavus Oppugno." He was calling on his dead ancestors to attack. Five spirits appeared in dark, gossamer form and charged Myros.

Then, from within the crowd, Baskor yelled, "Slayers, now." Hundreds of dragon slayers cast off their plebian robes revealing their Ellorian uniforms and celestine spears. They fired upon the Xyros, landing their Celestine lance points deep within the creature's necks. Thane stood motionless as Baskor attempted to seize Meligus. Baskor was thrown back by a simple wave of Meligus's hand. Myros was struggling to fight off the two-sided assault by the Saxeun ghosts and the dragons. She appeared to be weakening.

Tirous moved from the sidelines to directly protect Meligus, positioning himself between Meligus and the slayers. He knew that as soon as the dragons had been neutralized the slayers would go after Meligus. Tirous, though greatly outnumbered, began directly engaging with the slayers.

Meligus watched as Alyos moved into action, wielding the Forms, sending lightning bolts through the dragons. Meligus stared at Alyos and engaged the force of Axion. Alyos felt the power of the necromancer's spell beginning to work within his body, disassembling his body's structure. Sensing an imminent threat to Alyos I threw a significant piece of the broken pyramid stone at Meligus. It met its target and implanted itself on the side of his face. The force of Axion ceased. The rock's blow downed Meligus and he lay on the ground stunned.

Alyos moved closer to Myros and raised his hand. With his words, "Ctenophorus Subicio", he cast the closest dragon to the ground. As the dragon fell it spiraled downward past Alyos. With its left mouth open, two of its needle-like teeth caught Alyos's cheek, shredding it and taking a sizable chunk of skin with it. Alyos shrieked in agony as his flesh was ripped from his face. In utter rage Alyos screamed, "Drako Perniciem." All the dragons fell to the ground in one cataclysmic thunder, dead.

When Alyos wielded that Form I could feel the power of its energy reverberate through me. Wielding a form is controlled through will and intention. In his rage Alyos had lost his control and those words spread unconstrained, undirected, throughout the Earthlands. Totem fell from my shoulder, dead. With those words Alyos had destroyed the genus. He had killed all dragons. In the moments that followed every individual dragon of every species in all the Earthlands fell to the ground, dead. In times to come, our ancestors will relegate dragons to myth because of this moment. The genus Drako was no more. The profundity of the killing filled me with agony. Once again, the Formorian sister's words appeared before me, "The beasts will be banished from history's story."

Ailwin sensed what was happening as he felt the power of destruction flow through him and beyond. He screamed, "Alyos, No!"

Ailwin and I rode our horses through the crowd and dismounted onto the stage. In the midst of the bedlam, we stood before Meligus. The chaos was extreme; the toxic smell of acid, the thunder of the mega-stones crumbling to the earth, the dragons roaring with their assault and then plunging to their death, and the enlivened cadavers attacking Myros. I spoke first, "Meligus, your battle is with me. Stop this insanity and face me."

Meligus was processing what was unfolding; Thane refused to fight. Baskor had fooled and betrayed both of them. The Ellorians had prepared for the dragons. The Formorians had returned and the final battle was being fought just as Meligus reached the apex of his power. Ailwin joined Alyos and they turned their attention to protecting Myros. She was the lineage progenitor and was sacred to us. I faced Meligus alone.

He taunted me, "Simon, you could live in peace with your brother and mother. You could enjoy a quiet life of solitude but you chose this. Go and I will leave your family alone."

"Meligus," I answered. "Your words are never to be trusted. You wish me dead and the end to my lineage. I will end your reign the day it begins." I raised my hand and wielded the Form of Remembrance, "Anamnesis." Meligus's body shook and his face grimaced as he fought the memories flooding his mind.

Formorians are forbidden to alter a person's mind but we are permitted to allow remembrance. Meligus screamed as loving memories flooded his mind. In a desperate attempt to end the mental onslaught he shouted, "Orcus Mortem." He had summoned the dark beast of death from the underworld. This was not some ethereal, diaphanous, supernal ancestor. This was a beast from the Sheol of Gehenna Mons in the flesh. Its three-story form coalesced on the stage and its weight immediately crushed the stage beams, scattering all of us in the process. I rose, closing my eyes, becoming The Formless. Inside it was silent. In that instant the power inherent within the formless rose within me and, as I opened my eyes, that energy raged forth with a frightening force. Streaks of lightening emerged from my eyes, searing into the Orcus Mortem's flesh. With each flashing discharge of energy, thunder roared as the blasts ripped through the air. The beast absorbed impact after impact. Then, in a climactic discharge, I sent a final bolt into the beast ripping him apart with a deafening explosion. Bits of putrid, burnt flesh, blood and bone flew in all directions and splattered everyone in the vicinity.

Ailwin wielded one of the Forms of Suppression, "Reditus Infernum." He commanded the ghosts to return to the netherworlds from which they had been summoned. With Ailwin's banishment of the ancestral ghosts, the attack on Myros ended.

Meligus, sensing defeat, climbed onto one of the untethered horses and attempted to ride off. Tirous watched and also mounted a steed. Meligus looked back at Tirous and sensing the weight of his defeat said, "My best mate, for years you have lived in my shadow. It will now be left to you to bind the strength of the Earthlands."

The two pointed their horses north and whipped them attempting a precipitous escape. Alicia, running toward them, pulled back her bow and let her arrow fly. The arrowhead pierced Tirous's left ear auricle but that was not enough to end their withdrawal. Tirous let out a faint scream of pain and then spoke the words, "Evanescet Praetereo." Grey smoke engulfed the two escapees.

Alyos was not about to allow the one he blamed for his disfigurement and disgrace to escape. He mounted his horse and followed them into the grey fumes. His rage had not subsided and, as he rode toward the escapees, he whispered, "Perspicuitatem". His sibilant words cleared the air and made his prize visible. Meligus and Tirous now saw Alyos galloping toward them at full charge. Alyos, only yards from his prey, pulled back the reins, brought his horse to a full stop and spoke clearly, "Imprecatio Damnatio." With those forbidden words Alyos had damned the emperor to the hell worlds. Two grey soul eaters appeared as darkened clouds of evil. They converged upon Meligus, pulled him from his steed and lifted him into the air. The soul eaters ripped his soul from his physical body and Meligus's lifeless corpses fell to the ground as his spirit was taken to hell. Tirous screamed out his rage and rode off.

Ailwin and I, powerless to stop it, could only stand by helplessly as Alyos killed Meligus. Alyos rode back to confront us. "I am done respecting the confines the ancients imposed upon Formorian power. These petty, ungrateful humans will no longer spread their lies, rule with ignorance and inflict their pain upon me. I count you two as my friends but do not attempt to restrain or hinder me."

Ailwin quickly moved in front of Alyos and reached his hands toward Alyos's face. With both hands he grabbed Alyos's head and pushed his thumbs into his eyes. This was not intended to harm or blind Alyos but was done to directly install the power of the Formless into Alyos. Ailwin considered Alyos part of the lineage and, despite Alyos's rages and transgressions, Ailwin's compassion only wanted to help his friend. But Alyos responded with a tremendous blow that struck Ailwin's jaw sending the ancient seer crashing to the earth. Despite the shocking events that had transpired during the past hours this shocked me to my core. Rage was not a dominant part of my personality but seeing my master attacked was the final straw. Alyos had wielded the forbidden Forms, hurt Elloria and killed Meligus, but this was beyond the pale for me. My protective instincts rose to the forefront and from my depths the full power of the Formless passed through me. That immense force blasted forth upon Alyos and blew him to the ground disfiguring his body. Even though he lived, his face was drenched in his own blood issuing from the dragon's gashes incised into his face. His body lay immovable. I acted quickly to help Ailwin.

Surrcon, who had just witnessed the death of his beloved son, emerged from the crowd seeking Alyos. Alyos had no strength to resist as Surrcon grabbed him by the hair and spoke softly, "Lateo." With that enchantment the two vanished.

I moved Ailwin under the shade of the nearest tree. Baskor and Alicia, witnessing Alyos's attack on Ailwin, rushed over to assess his condition. It was obvious from the bone jutting from his jaw that Ailwin's recovery would take some time. This was to be his final battle and the defining moment of his retirement. He looked affectionately at me and spoke, "The duty to maintain the Balance is now solely yours Simon." I gently touched his jaw and quietly uttered, "Sana." Ailwin's jaw began to heal.

Ailwin patted my shoulder and asked, "Did Surrcon take Alyos?" I nodded in the affirmative. Ailwin responded, "Now a new history may be forged and the overlord shall rise."

Alicia and Baskor climbed to the top of one of the mega-stones in order to find high-ground from which to address the stunned crowd. Baskor shouted an order to the dragon slayers, "Arrest Thane." The troops closest to the crumbled stage grasped Thane's arms and took him into custody.

Alicia addressed the throng. "Recent history has been manipulated and falsified. Meligus and Thane have distorted the truth and you, my people, have been deceived." She then turned to Thane and ordered him to speak. "Thane, tell them the truth."

Thane hesitated but the two guards who were holding him jerked his arms painfully behind his back and he relented. "Meligus and I captured the chimera and released them into the cities. Meligus allowed the destruction to unfold and then destroyed the beasts when they had finished ravaging you and your cities. He spun his lies in order to become emperor and destroy the reputation of the Formorians. I assisted him in his plan. I beg my monarch's, my brother's and your forgiveness." Then Thane broke down and wept.

Alicia continued, addressing the crowd, "The time for deception, destruction and darkness ends now. We have a chance at unification, a chance to live in support of each other. The three city-states may retain their uniqueness but we have an opportunity to thrive together." The crowd stood silent, their allegiances having been whipsawed, manipulated and strained to the limits. What was clear was the people wanted to return to a peaceful surety and normalcy. Alicia was to be the warrantor of that.

Cardinal Gregory never received the farmlands of Calfore. He was forced to rescind his writ of excommunication against me. Alicia and Baskor returned to Elloria as co-regents. Thane was imprisoned. I accompanied Ailwin back to the Glacier Mountains helping him settle into his retirement and the Formless. Soon after, I returned to Themos where Omnesta and I oversaw the repairs to the Myros pyramid and the operations of the conservatory and temple. The Formorian students returned to their studies. I searched for Alyos but he and Surrcon remained hidden. The world returned to an uneasy normalcy.

But things had changed. Honor was no longer automatically afforded to the gentry. Stature was no longer automatically bestowed upon the wealthy. Faith was no longer automatically conferred upon the church. In private, dogma was questioned. Inwardly, the serf no longer saw himself as a possession. Secretly, the uneducated no longer saw themselves as ignorant. Worth and station were being quietly transformed. It was not a revolution or cataclysm. It was subtle and delicate, yet pervasive. The chasm between the low and the high might now be traversable. It seemed as though there was a new balance emerging.

But, in my mind, there was that nagging phrase uttered years before by the Formorian sister, *"The Balance will tarnish, bereft of its glory."*

About The Author

James Pesavento spent decades in the frantic world of commodity trading while, at the same time, being a meditation teacher. Writing has been his passion for many years and now, in the form of The True History of Dragons and Wizards, he brings together fun, adventure and the unexpected, revealing what truly happened during the time of darkness. 'The Lord of Forms' begins the hair-raising adventure and, in the sequel, The Spawn of the Hellkite, he continues to reveal the treachery, battles and revenge that shook the Earthlands in this tumultuous time.